Emperor Ai

Harlowe Savage

Monarchs of EROS

HARLOWE SAVAGE

Thank You

This is for all you Notorious Bisexuals out there.

Harlowe

1

Chapter One

Light trickled in through the window slats as Dong Xian opened his eyes and stretched, the blankets falling to the wayside. He could hear the sounds of Lihua shuffling around in the kitchen, preparing the day's breakfast. Dong swung his legs down over the edge of the bed, his feet brushing the slippers that were left by the bedside the night before. Today was an incredibly important day, today was the day that Dong began his government duties as a minor official inside the palace.

For the last several years, Dong had been working as a minor government official on a purely local level, handling things such as disputes between villagers, tax collection, and managing the books. It had been absolutely riveting (read: incredibly boring). However, Dong was excited to move up in the world, to bigger and better things. Just last week he'd been approached by the local governor with a proposition; a position in the imperial palace had just opened up, and given his seniority on the local level, the promotion had been offered to him. Ecstatic to have the opportunity to explore the, typically off limits, palace, Dong had jumped at the chance.

Of course, it would mean that he would be home considerably less than usual, but he didn't think that would be too much of an issue. He and Lihua had gotten married five years ago and while she was a wonderful wife in title, they didn't really have much in common. Every morning, she would get up and make them breakfast, lay out his clothing, and see him off, but Dong got the feeling that the weekends he went on business trips were his wife's favorite time of each month. The mornings he would leave, Lihua would have an elaborate and labor intensive breakfast set out for him and just seem to be in higher spirits. Then, when he would return, there was a brief period of time when Dong would witness his wife in a state of relaxation before they fell back into their typical routine, at which time she would slip back into the standard wifely demeanor he had come to know her by. Honor, tradition, and reverent respect.

Meandering over to the dressing area, Dong saw that Lihua had laid out his best robe along with a hair ribbon that she had given him as a gift upon hearing about his promotion. It was black and sleek, made of cotton, and embroidered on the sides with gold thread. The rest of his ensemble was also black with golden embroidery. Lihua had made the ribbon specifically to go with this outfit, stating that he couldn't possibly visit the imperial palace regularly without at least one fully put together ensemble.

Lihua had braided his hair the night before and put it up in such a way that it wouldn't get messy as he slept on it, so all Dong had to do was tie the ribbon to the end of his hair to cover up the plainer, more standard ribbon that was used the night before.

"No, you can't sleep with the black ribbon in your hair." She'd said. "It would get wrinkled and look unfitting of an official, especially if you were to run into the Emperor."

She was right he supposed, but in the back of his mind, Dong wondered to himself what the chances of him actually running into the Emperor were. The Emperor was a busy man and only a few years older than himself, he was still learning everything he could about the best ways to run the government with the assistance of the Three Counselors of State. The Three Counselors of State were made up of the Chancellor, the Great Secretary, and the Grand Commandant.

The Chancellor was primarily responsible for creating and managing the government budget, conversely, the Secretary's duty was to conduct and oversee disciplinary proceedings for government officials, and the Grand Commandant was the commander of the military in the place of the Emperor. Dong wouldn't need to interact too much with the Grand Commandant, as he was still to be a low ranking government official, primarily responsible for local administrative affairs. However, the Chancellor was the one who appointed him and if he caused any trouble, the Secretary would be the man he would face.

Dong made a quick promise to himself to not cause any issues in the palace. The last thing he needed was to piss off the very people who appointed him in the first place.

After donning his robe and gently tying the ribbon to the bottom of his braid, Dong meandered out into the kitchen where, sure enough, Lihua was at work serving the food she had made onto plates for the two of them at the table. At his approach, Lihua lifted her gaze before bowing her head down once again.

"Good morning Jahng-foo," Lihua greeted him, gesturing for him to kneel at the table and eat. "Breakfast is ready."

Dong nodded and sat at the table cross legged as Lihua knelt and sat with her feet tucked underneath her. His wife poured them tea and served each of them in silence before finally speaking as Dong began to eat.

"First day at the palace."

"Yes," Dong replied, making a noise of approval at the delicious bite he'd taken. "Today we'll be sticking primarily to introductions, the real work won't actually begin until tomorrow."

Lihua nodded and made a small noise of acknowledgment. "Well, I made you a midday meal regardless, as I know you will likely still be traveling and won't arrive at the palace until this evening."

Dong smiled gently. "Thank you."

He and Lihua had an arranged marriage, as most were. Dong recognized that he'd been incredibly lucky to receive someone of Lihua's caliber, especially in the small province in which they lived. Coming to live together as strangers had been about as initially uncomfortable as one would expect, but over the years, Dong liked to believe that they had formed a nice relationship based on mutual respect and kindness to one another. Every day, Lihua would cook for them, go to the market to purchase ingredients for dinner and breakfast for the next day, wash the clothes, and keep the home clean. Dong, on the other hand, would go to work, and on the occasion that he went out of town, he would always be sure to bring something nice back for his wife, whether that was a bracelet, hairpin, or bolt of cloth.

Dong hadn't felt uncomfortable around his wife in quite some time and he would like to think that she did not feel uncomfortable around him either.

"Breakfast is delicious as always," Dong complimented as he finished his soup.

"Thank you Jahng-foo," Lihua responded, a small smile playing at the corner of her mouth.

"Is there anything that you would like from the markets in Chang'an?" Dong asked, finishing up the vegetables and rice left on his plate.

"I do not need anything," Lihua replied, as she always did when he asked. However, Dong had known her long enough to know that this first refusal was more out of politeness than anything else.

"I know you do not," Dong replied. "But I would like to purchase something for you in the capital and I would hate to get you something that you would not like. So, truthfully, you would be doing me a service by telling me what you would want."

Lihua's lips tilted up in a little smile. "Well, if you insist."

"I do."

"I had been hoping to get my hands on some fabric that we are unlikely to stumble upon here, anything new would do nicely. I was hoping to make you some new clothes since you will be traveling to the capital more frequently. I also thought that I could make myself some new clothes as well in the off chance that I ever need to accompany you."

"That sounds like a great idea." Dong nodded. He placed his chopsticks down and Lihua immediately moved to begin clearing the table. "I will be back in a week."

Lihua hummed in response and turned to bow as Dong began making his way to the door. "Travel safely."

Dong smiled and nodded, replacing his slippers with shoes and stepping out into the morning. He began making his way to the end of the street where a carriage was awaiting him. Upon arrival, the driver bowed his head and opened the door.

"Ah, Dong. There you are." Yang Xiong was nose deep in a scroll but rolled it back up and placed it to the side as Dong entered the carriage. Dong was lucky that his friend happened to be heading to the capital this very morning or he would have likely had to ride the full way on horseback. It wasn't an unreasonable thing to do, as many people made the trip frequently, but he was still grateful to his friend since the long journey would be far more comfortable in the carriage.

"I see that Lihua made you lunch for the trip."

"Ah yes." Dong smiled to himself, placing the wrapped box on the seat next to him. "She is very attentive, though I think she's mostly just excited to get me out of town for a week."

Yang snorted and crossed his legs in the seat. "Perhaps, but you're very lucky that you have a wife that cares if you go hungry on a long journey or not. Feiyan could not be fucked one way or another to care if I should happen to die of starvation on one of my trips."

"Oh, come on now." Dong chuckled. "I'm sure that's not true."

"But it is!" Yang protested. "She's a horrible woman. Honestly, one of the primary reasons I travel so much is so that I don't need to see her every day. Sure, she makes breakfast and cleans the house but, I swear Dong, when we eat in the mornings I can feel her eyes boring through my skull and I can almost hear her praying that I choke."

Dong chuckled. "I'm sure it's not all bad."

Yang shook his head and sighed. "You're right. Sometimes she sleeps in the guest bedroom and I get to sleep peacefully without her frigid devil feet touching me in the middle of the night."

Dong couldn't help but crack a smile as the carriage began to move.

Yang rattled on about the stresses and daily frustrations of being at home while flipping through the scrolls he'd brought. Dong eventually tuned him out, just making a noncommittal noise every so often to maintain the illusion that he was still involved in the conversation. He and Yang had been friends since they were children and he was very used to the other man's rants. It was no surprise to him that he had decided to become a scholar; Yang could talk until his face was blue and then still continue until he lost consciousness. Dong got the impression that one of the reasons his wife didn't like him very much was because he never let her get a word in edgewise, but he'd never mention that to him.

Their province was a small one and Dong didn't really have many friends even at 19. He'd been made an official earlier that year but he knew that it wasn't due to his political prowess or really any other sort of talent he possessed. The truth of the matter was that very few people actually wanted to do the job, so when it was offered to him, he accepted partly as a favor to his father's friend who'd offered.

It wasn't like he knew very much about politics, but he did try. Part of the reason he was so nervous to visit the capital and participate in conversations in the palace was because of his lack of experience. He did, however, hope to absorb some expertise from the myriad of political men that he would be in contact with on a daily basis. Who knows? Maybe he would even get to learn from the Emperor himself.

Dong didn't know too much about the Emperor aside from what he'd been told by the province's head official.

Emperor Ai was 20 years old, only a year older than himself, and was intelligent, articulate, and capable. Officials had been incredibly excited about his ascension earlier in the year, stating that he would be a perfect fit for the position. Dong found himself wondering what sort of person this Emperor was; what books he'd read, how long he studied each day to be an effective political leader, and what sort of resolve he had to be this accomplished at only one year older than himself.

Dong liked reading, but that hadn't truly served him in his position as much as he hoped it would. He thoroughly enjoyed works of fiction and poetry, often preferring to spend his days copying over his favorite poems and committing them to memory as opposed to reading the dry government instructional books he was meant to. It wasn't that he didn't care, it was just that there wasn't too much happening in his little province anyway, so the likelihood of him needing to know the different types of military actions he could take should an attack occur on his village were slim to none.

The carriage bumped and rattled as the pair passed fields and fields of rice, the workers bent over in the water. Dong supposed he should be more grateful for his position as it disqualified him from working jobs requiring hard labor like those of the rice paddy workers. Tuning Yang back in, Dong nodded along as his friend rattled off some of the musings of a philosopher he'd been reading up on recently and tried his best to pay attention, letting the rice paddy fields pass him by.

2

Chapter Two

The rest of the journey was incredibly uneventful. In fact, Dong found himself dozing off on more than one occasion. He ate his lunch, which was delicious as it always was, and even found that Lihua had packed enough for both of them. Yang was very grateful and Dong made himself a mental note to buy her something nice at the markets in addition to the fabrics as thanks. After a little while longer, Dong dozed off and didn't come to until the smell of cooking meat hit his nose.

He blinked his eyes open and stretched, looking out the window again.

"Have a nice nap?" Yang asked, an amused smile playing on his lips. Yang had immersed himself in his scrolls again, putting a temporary end to his ramblings.

"I did, thank you," Dong responded, looking out the window again. "Remind me to invite you over to our home on nights I'm having trouble sleeping. Your storytelling always seems to do the trick."

"Oh, fuck off," Yang shot back, shoving his scrolls back into his bag. Dong grinned and turned his attention to the scenery outside the carriage window. The endless fields of rice had melted away and had been replaced with the busy streets of the capital, the meat that Dong had been smelling was coming from one of the many carts lining the road.

"Different, isn't it?" Yang prompted.

He was absolutely correct, while the streets of their province were filled with farmers and children playing with dogs, these were absolutely bustling with people from all walks of life; merchants, grocers, nobles, everyone seemed to have business with someone in the city.

"Very." Dong replied breathlessly.

Too soon, however, the marketplace streets gave way to the private road leading up to the palace and Dong's excitement was replaced with a nervous fluttering. He'd hitched a ride with Yang for the sake of convenience, but technically his political duties didn't require him to be here until tomorrow. Of course, he wouldn't be the only arrival that night, but since Yang was speaking at a conference later that evening, he would have a great deal of time on his hands and no one to spend it with. Yang shrugged at his concern and smiled, gathering up his things from the carriage.

"Just take the time to explore the palace grounds. It's truly a beautiful building and you never know when you'll have the chance to just meander about once your political duties start."

So, this was how Dong found himself wandering through the most beautiful gardens he'd ever seen. Upon arrival at the palace, some servants had shown him to his room and after making himself comfortable, he set out to do some exploring. Hooking a right just outside of his chamber doors, Dong began to follow a path that wound in a serpentine fashion through the palace gardens. The Ixora chinensis was in bloom so everywhere he looked, little bundles of orange flowers swayed in the wind, and a little further down the pathway Dong stumbled across a bed of pink peonies. Lily pads floated atop the peaceful ponds, flashes of the orange and white koi making an appearance every now and then.

Dong was convinced that he would be content to wander the gardens forever when something caught his eye. Just up the pathway were a set of open doors leading into a well lit room, in one of the corners Dong saw a stack of scrolls that had been set aside for some purpose and left to return to later. This was enough to pique his interest, there were only so many books and scrolls that he had access to in his province, so the potential for access to more was enough for him to alter his course and wander into the space.

It became apparent very quickly, to Dong's excitement, that this was one of the, presumably many, libraries in the palace. Shelves lined the walls, creating walkways throughout the room, and every last one of them was filled with books and scrolls. Dong wandered into one of the book-laden alleyways and began skimming through the titles on the shelves. Most of these were historical texts, and Dong pouted a little to himself before setting off through the rows of shelves again in search of something a little lighter. If he could find a nice book of poetry, he would find a spot in the gardens and keep himself occupied for the rest of the evening and likely most of the next morning until the meetings were due to start.

As he wandered, he came upon a break in the rows of shelves. In the middle was a table, covered in scrolls and stacks upon stacks of books, but that was not what gave him pause. Also at the table, head down on his arm was a man. He had long, black hair that was half tied up in a knot on the top of his head, the rest of it cascading down his shoulders. He was likely another noble here for the assembly, Dong thought. His robes were far too nice to just be a politician from a satellite province like himself.

Sun trickled through the windows and onto his face illuminating how long his eyelashes were. Dong watched as the man's shoulders rose and fell with his breath, a stray piece of hair falling across his face. He almost felt like he was intruding but he couldn't bring himself to walk away, the man had some sort of magnetic pull and so he stood there watching, for how long he did not know. Dong let his gaze trail over the graceful curvature of the man's shoulder and down his nose to his plump lips, slightly parted in sleep.

He felt his cheeks begin to blush slightly as he admired them, however, that train of thought was quickly disrupted by the sound of a closing door. Dong jumped and turned to face the direction that the noise had come from; the owner of the pile of books and scrolls he had seen earlier had come to return to them. He took a breath and turned back, unexpectedly meeting the gaze of the beautiful and now very awake, man. Their eyes met and Dong opened and closed his mouth a couple of times as if contemplating whether or not he should apologize for staring. Ultimately, however, he grabbed a random book off the shelf next to him and walked quickly down the aisle, leaving the table area behind.

As he turned the corner, he pressed his back up against the shelf and held the book tightly to his chest. He breathed through his nose to slow his heart which was, for some reason, beating like a hummingbird's. The blush on his cheeks remained and he stood there for a moment collecting himself, from what, he was not sure. He peered around the corner and chanced a glance down the aisle, to the open area. However, the man was no longer sitting amongst his pile of books. Dong looked around in confusion and began to step quietly down the aisle, keeping an eye out for the man.

He really should leave, Dong thought. Getting caught staring at a stranger while he was sleeping was bad enough, he really didn't need to get caught returning to the scene of the crime for another glimpse. Yet, he couldn't help himself as he continued through the towering walls of books.

Carefully, Dong leaned around the corner, looking left and right for the man but saw absolutely no one. Just the pile of books on the table, with the chair pushed out. Dong sighed and relaxed a little, maybe he'd just imagined the man sitting there; it had been a long day of travel.

"Looking for something?" A deep voice came from behind him.

Dong startled and turned on his heel, finding himself nose to nose with the beautiful stranger. His eyelashes were even longer up close and gods did he smell nice.

"Um." Dong began smartly, gaze flitting rapidly between the other man's gem-like eyes. The stranger tilted his head and stepped a little closer, a coy smile playing on his lips. "I was just..." Dong gestured helplessly at the shelves on either side of them. "Browsing."

"Browsing." The other man parroted back with amusement in his voice. He was at least a head taller than Dong was, if not more, and his ebony black hair reached down to his waist.

"Yes," Dong whispered. No matter how much he tried, he could not bring himself to look away from the dark gaze trapping him in place. "I um... just got in and I was... uh." Dong couldn't help but glance quickly down at the man's mouth. What was *wrong* with him?

"Browsing." The man finished for him, a smile breaking through.

"Yes." Dong replied breathlessly. "Browsing."

"Well." Thankfully for Dong's heart, the man stepped back, leaning against the opposite bookcase. "Find anything worth reading?"

Suddenly Dong remembered that he was holding a book in his hands and he grinned, holding it up. "Yep. I'm excited to read some new poetry."

The stranger's eyebrows went up and his eyes bounced over to the book in Dong's hand and then back to meet his gaze.

"Well, you won't find any in there." The man replied teasingly.

Glancing down at the book in his hand, he felt his stomach drop as he read the title, *Parthian Stations, a geography of trade routes in Parthia.*

Shit.

"Oh, um…" Dong laughed awkwardly and let his hands fall to his side. "I suppose not."

Suddenly, the man was moving towards him again and Dong swallowed, head tilting up as he approached. He gently took the book out of Dong's hand and turned, gesturing for him to follow.

"Try this instead." The stranger placed *Parthian Stations* down on the table along with his myriad of other books and instead picked up a smaller, cloth-bound book and handed it over to Dong. "I find that the poems in this one are much nicer."

Dong took the book in his hands and ran his thumbs over the cover. On the front of the book, in beautiful penmanship read "Eternities with You".

"Thank you." Dong swallowed and smiled softly at the man. "I will make sure to bring it back before I leave."

"Please do." The stranger responded, gaze soft. "It's one of my favorites."

Dong nodded and looked back down at the book, he was about to ask the stranger his name when someone else walked into the library, breaking their little bubble.

"Ai." The voice called. The stranger turned his head and clearly recognizing the intruder, nodded and turned his attention back to Dong.

"Well, I will see you around." Ai said before turning and making his way through the stacks of books before disappearing around a corner.

Ai... that's a nice name.

Dong wandered back out to the gardens after he'd taken some time to recover from his interaction with the beautiful stranger. However, by the time he made his way outside, Ai and the intruder were long gone.

Sitting down on a bench near the peonies he'd seen earlier, Dong pulled out the book and opened the cover, turning to the first page.

All my love.

The author had written.

Until I meet you again under the stars in our next life.

Dong felt his face begin to burn again, Ai had given him a book of love poems. He placed one of his palms on his cheek to soak up some of the heat and turned the page.

In the quiet gardens
The voice, like a song
Penetrates my heart
And calls to my soul.
I know not, to whom it belongs

But I know now,
That I can never live without it.

Dong bit his lip and traced his fingertips over the page. Most of the poetry books in his collection were copies of the poems by the greats; he'd read them so many times he knew every single line, but this was different. This was a book of poems written by someone nameless for the love of their life. It was intimate, fragile, and beautiful.

As Dong flipped through the pages, he noted that every single page was hand transcribed and carefully written, not by a scribe who copied the letters again and again, but by a single person, in their own style. He gently closed the cover again and looked around, even though it was futile, Ai and his friend were long gone but caught up in the romance of the poems he looked anyway, just in case.

The sun had begun to set and despite his efforts to look, there wasn't another soul in the gardens with him. Standing, Dong tucked the book carefully into his arms and began the walk back to his quarters. Tomorrow would be the start of a very long day and he needed to get some rest.

Morning came far too quickly for Dong's liking; despite knowing that the day would be packed full of duties to fulfill and political conversations to be had, he couldn't help but stay up and read by the light of the candle. Eventually, he fell asleep, but when the servants came in to wake him, he knew that he'd definitely stayed up far too late reading.

As he dressed, he thought back to his meeting with Ai in the library and how lovely he'd looked sleeping there on the table, his head on his arm. It was likely that he would never see Ai again, the palace was huge and he was only here for a week. In addition to that, the week would be filled with back to back conferences, meetings, and meals with other politicians, so there wouldn't really be any time for him to slip away. He would just have to continue reading the book before he went to sleep and leave the potential of another meeting up to fate.

Dong sighed as he made his way out of the chambers and into the hallway.

"Dong." A booming voice echoed through the hall and Dong turned around to see a familiar face.

"Good morning Governor Li." Dong bowed respectfully and waited for his counterpart to catch up.

Zhou Li was a jovial man in his 50's who happened to be the current Governor of Dong's province. In fact, Governor Li had been the person who nominated Dong for his position of office in the first place. Zhou Li and his father had been friends growing up and when Dong's father passed away, Governor Li had been quick to step in and help his mother take care of him and his sister.

"I wasn't aware that you were coming in this morning." The Governor said, initiating conversation, leading them down the hallway.

"I didn't." Dong responded. "I arrived last night, I hitched a ride with Yang, he is speaking at some sort of conference in the city over the next couple of days."

Governor Li nodded, pursing his lips approvingly. "That makes sense. It is quite the long journey to the capital from home."

Dong nodded back. "How's your wife?"

Governor Li chuckled and clasped his hands behind his back as they walked. "Daiyu is doing quite well, thank you for asking. She tells me that she misses me terribly when I'm away on trips like this but she certainly appreciates the gifts I bring back every time."

Dong smiled and glanced over his shoulder as they passed an open window leading out to the gardens. There were a couple of servant women tending to the flowers and trimming the bushes and trees but no sign of Ai. He hadn't expected to see him, but he still couldn't help but look.

"I'm sure Lihua feels the same way." Governor Li continued.

"Well." Dong grinned softly. "I don't think she'd ever tell me to my face but I think she probably likes her alone time at the house. One less person to clean up after and more time for her to work on her hobbies."

Governor Li's booming laugh echoed through the chamber as they approached the building they were heading for.

"That's wives for you I suppose."

"Yes. I suppose it is." Dong replied.

"I heard an interesting tidbit of information when I was heading in this morning."

"Oh?" The doors to the dining hall opened and the pair made their way inside.

"I heard that the Emperor is going to make an appearance at this week's talks."

"Is that what you heard?" Dong replied.

"Yes and I don't think you fully comprehend what a huge deal that is."

Governor Li took a look around the room, waving at some other gentlemen sitting at a table in the corner and changing their course to head in that direction.

"This is the first meeting of leaders that the Emperor will be attending since his coronation."

Dong hummed in interest as they sat.

"I've heard great things about him and I'm interested to see where he falls on the spectrum of issues we've gathered to discuss."

Governor Li turned in his seat and tilted his head so that he could speak softly to Dong. "Don't worry too much, I know this is your first meeting too. Just sit back and observe today, you will get a better idea of how these things run and will then be better prepared for the rest of the week."

Dong let out a breath that he didn't realize he was holding and grinned at his mentor. He parted his lips to thank him when horns drew the attention of the whole group to a pair of double doors opening in the back of the room. Quickly, Governor Li and the rest of the officials got up to bow at a ninety degree angle and Dong scrambled to do the same.

"His Imperial Majesty." A voice rang through the corridor. "Emperor Ai of Han."

Ai…

Dong's thoughts immediately jumped back to yesterday in the library and he bit his lip as he stared at the floor. Now was not the time nor the place to be thinking about the handsome stranger who'd given him a book of love poems just the day prior. It was one hell of a coincidence though, that they'd have the same name.

Dong lifted his gaze, following the lead of Li beside him, and immediately felt his mouth go dry. Because standing there in front of him, dressed in luxurious golden robes, a crown perched on his head, was Ai, the beautiful stranger.

3

Chapter Three

Dong blinked a couple of times, shaking his head slightly, convinced that this was some sort of strange trick of the light. This couldn't possibly be real, there was no way that the Emperor of China had given him a book of love poems yesterday.

Dong felt his heart skip a beat because Ai... the Emperor, chose that exact moment to look over in his direction. Their eyes met and Dong could feel his face begin to heat up; he could swear that he saw the Emperor's lips twitch up in a smile but he couldn't be sure. Before he knew it, Governor Li was tugging at his sleeve, indicating for him to sit. Clumsily he sat back down, breaking eye contact and he was positive that when he looked back up, the Emperor's gaze would have moved on, but upon raising his gaze, he was met with the same striking eyes.

Dong swallowed the best he could and tried his best not to stare, but it was useless. The Emperor's gaze on him felt like a gravitational pull, he was incapable of looking away. His heart fluttered and he thought back to a poem he'd read late last night as he was falling asleep.

Lightning strikes

Again

But I cannot see

Suspended forever in eternity,

With you.

Then after what could have been a couple of seconds or several days, the moment passed and the Emperor's attention shifted to the woman sitting at his side. Finally, Dong felt like he could breathe again.

"What was that about?" Dong startled as Governor Li whispered over his shoulder.

"Um... nothing." Dong murmured back. "I just recognize him, that's all."

Dong chanced a look at Governor Li and was met with a confused expression.

"I thought you'd never been to the capital before."

"I haven't." Dong replied. "I got here last night and did some exploring of the palace. I met him in the library, I didn't know he was the Emperor though."

"Well." Li mumbled as the palace concubines made their way around the table with tea. "Let's hope you weren't too terribly informal with him."

Dong's face flushed again as he remembered how close they'd been when Ai had come up behind him in the library.

"I don't know why he wouldn't tell you that he was the Emperor at the time." Governor Li mused.

"Yeah, neither do I." Dong's gaze drifted back up to the front of the hall. Emperor Ai was engaged in conversation with a couple of the other officials in attendance and Dong took the moment to observe him. The way he held himself was essentially the same as the day before, the only major differences were in the robes and crown he wore on his head.

Oh, gods. Panic rushed through Dong's veins like an ice bath. He'd been spying on the Emperor of China while he was taking a nap in his private library. He'd only been an official for six months and he'd already fucked it up.

Dong took a deep breath and stared at the hands in his lap. He might as well enjoy his first and last meal as a government official before he was sent packing back to Lihua. The rest of the meal went by fairly uneventfully as Dong tried to continue to engage in conversation with Li and the other Governors. He could swear that he could almost feel the Emperor's eyes on him throughout the entire ordeal, but he didn't dare sneak a peek. With any luck, the Emperor would completely forget about him and he would fly under the radar for the rest of the week.

After the meal ended, Dong excused himself to the restroom and made his way down a long hallway just outside of the dining hall. He stopped just short of the restroom and braced himself on the banister, looking out into the gardens. A small breeze blew through his hair and rustled his robes as he took another deep breath. His plan seemed to be working pretty well at this point, nobody had pulled him aside or called him out. He just needed to keep his nose to the ground, do his job, and try not to cause any incidents.

"Avoiding me?" Dong jumped at the familiar, deep voice behind him. He spun on his heel, back against the banister and once again found himself face to face with the beautiful stranger, who he now knew to be Emperor Ai. Dong looked from side to side for his entourage, settling back on the Emperor's face when he found no one.

"I... no." Dong bit his bottom lip and prayed that the Emperor wouldn't see through his clear deception. Causing his heart to jump in his chest again, Emperor Ai stepped forward, closer into his space.

"Why so jumpy?" Ai asked, smirking slightly.

"Why didn't you tell me you were the Emperor yesterday?" Dong couldn't help himself as the question spilled from his lips. Internally he was kicking himself, who was he to question why the Emperor did anything? Externally he wasn't faring much better, a blush spreading across his face. Dong averted his gaze, staring at the Emperor's shoes as his own feet shuffled awkwardly. After a few beats, Dong realized that the Emperor wasn't responding and he raised his head back up to apologize, but Ai just smiled when their eyes met.

"Because I figured you might react like this." Emperor Ai chuckled and moved to stand next to Dong instead of immediately in front of him. Dong chewed on his bottom lip, ever aware of the other man's presence. "I was curious about you yesterday and I wanted to talk without my identity ruining our interaction."

Dong felt his eyebrows scrunch in confusion and before he could think about what he was going to say, his head was already turning.

"Why?" The second that the word made its way past his lips, Dong felt himself heating up again in embarrassment. Here he was, questioning the Emperor again. What was wrong with him?

"You intrigue me." Ai was watching Dong like he was curious to see what he would do next. Dong wasn't sure if he felt like he was being watched with the curious eyes of one who wanted to observe him or the predatory gaze of someone who wanted to eat him. There was something hungry in the Emperor's gaze that Dong couldn't quite place, but it ignited a fire in his stomach that he was unfamiliar with. This time Dong didn't tear his gaze away, but instead watched the Emperor in return, studying his face. When he didn't find any sort of dishonesty or joking nature in his expression, Dong pursed his lips and made a noise of interest.

"I don't know why." Dong turned his gaze back out to the gardens, aware that the Emperor's eyes were still on him. "I'm not very interesting." Dong laughed half-heartedly.

"I disagree."

Dong turned his attention back to the Emperor, surprised at the response.

"I find you very interesting." Dong's grip tightened on the banister as his breathing picked up slightly. This was very new for him, being on the receiving end of this amount of honest attention. The bubble was broken once again, however when horns rang out.

"We should be getting back I suppose." Dong murmured.

"Yes." Emperor Ai replied, stepping back away from the banister and placing his hands behind his back. "We should."

Dong swallowed, still placing his weight on his palms, holding himself up by the banister. Emperor Ai turned his head towards the direction the horns had come from and Dong couldn't help but stare at his jawline, sharp, manly, and absolutely handsome.

"After, however." Ai spoke again, turning back and Dong immediately diverted his eyes back up to the Emperor's, away from his jawline. "Have Mei Lan show you to my quarters."

Dong felt the Emperor's gaze on him, heavy and intense.

"I would like to finish this conversation." Emperor Ai turned again and began walking back towards the dining hall before stopping and looking back over his shoulder. "I also can't wait to hear what you think about the book."

It took Dong several minutes after the Emperor had walked away to regain his sense of being and realize that he needed to be heading back as well. Blushing, Dong thought about the smirk Ai had been wearing as he turned back to speak to him again. Was the Emperor flirting with him?

Dong stayed behind as Governor Li and the other politicians took their leave, excusing that he wanted to wander the gardens again before their conference later that evening, feeling that some fresh air would do him and his nerves some good. Technically it wasn't a lie, he would be walking around outside and the air would be good for his nerves. He just wasn't nervous because of the conference, nor was he just wandering the gardens without a specific destination in mind.

Once everyone cleared out, Dong approached a woman that he assumed to be Mei Lan and she showed him to a much nicer area of the palace. Nobody really paid too much attention to him since he was being escorted, but Dong couldn't help but feel like everyone was staring at him because he didn't belong. Though soon enough they arrived at the Emperor's quarters and Mei Lan opened the doors for him before stepping back and bowing.

Dong waited for her to lead the way, but when it became abundantly clear that she was not going to be accompanying him, he swallowed nervously and made his way inside. The Emperor's quarters were as lavish and incredible as anything that he would have been able to conjure up in his mind. Every wall was decorated with tapestries, every surface laden with ornate vases and bronze statuettes. Dong heard the great double doors close behind him and he continued into the space, approaching another set of open doors. The room had an entire wall that was open to the gardens, overlooking the palace grounds, and there, standing with his back to Dong was Emperor Ai.

Ai seemed to hear him approaching as he turned slightly, beckoning with his head for Dong to come closer. Mustering all the courage he had, Dong strode across the room and joined Ai on the balcony.

"The poems in the book are beautiful." Dong tried, glancing at the Emperor from his peripheral vision. His heart clenched when a demure smile appeared on the Emperor's lips.

"I'm glad you liked them." Emperor Ai tilted his head to look in Dong's direction. "It's one of my favorite books of poetry. Growing up I was expected to be well read in the classics in addition to my military and political studies, but these poems were just something I kept for myself."

"I can understand that." Dong played with his fingers, switching between looking directly at Ai and out into the gardens. "We didn't have very many books in our province when I was growing up so whenever I could get my hands on one, I would bring it home and read it over and over until the cover was worn and broken in."

Dong smiled to himself, finding his body relaxing a little. "I remember the first time that one of the traveling merchants had a book of poetry. Of course, I bought it with the little money I had from doing odd jobs around the village before I even knew what kind of book it was. But when I opened it, I was so intrigued by the contents. It was nothing like any of the books that my father had given me about the history of the area, nor was it like the ones my mother had containing her recipes."

Dong shifted, remembering the first poem he'd ever memorized from that book.

"On this lucky day, good in both its signs," Dong recited.

Let us in reverence give pleasure to the Monarch on high.

I hold my long sword by its jade grasp;

My girdle-gems tinkle with a Ch'iu-ch'iang.

From the jewelled mat with its jade weights

Why not now take the perfumed spray?

Meats I offer, flavoured with basil, on strewn orchids laid;

I set out the cassia-wine and peppered drink.

Now the sticks are raised, the drums are struck,

To beats distanced and slow the chanters gently sing,

Then to the ranks of reed-organ and zither make loud reply.

The Spirit moves proudly in his splendid gear;

Sweetest scents with gusts of fragrance fill the hall.

The five notes chime in thick array...

"The Lord is pleased and happy, his heart at rest." Emperor Ai chimed in with the final line. "The Songs of Chu, the first of the Nine Songs, I'm impressed."

Dong flushed slightly, realizing that he'd gotten lost in his reminiscing. "Don't be." Dong chuckled. "In provinces like mine, I didn't have much else to do with my time. At one point I probably had the entire book memorized, though I'm not sure that I'd be able to remember all of it now if asked."

"I don't know about that." Ai replied sounding amused. "I find that we are capable of far more than we give ourselves credit for."

Dong turned to comment on that train of thought but found himself speechless as Ai had moved closer, into Dong's immediate space. Subconsciously, Dong licked his lips, his eyes flitting up and down between the Emperor's eyes and mouth.

"I think." The Emperor continued, "That you are capable of more than you give yourself credit for."

It was all Dong could do to continue breathing normally and ignore the growing interest between his legs. Ai reached out and brushed his thumb over Dong's jawline, sending a shiver through his whole body. Dong felt his eyes drifting closed and having the reaction he was likely looking for elicited, Ai leaned in, his breath dancing on the other man's lips, giving him a chance to pull away should he choose. When he did not, Dong felt a soft pair of lips press to his and let out a breath through his nose, relaxing into it.

Ai's hand moved from Dong's jaw to the back of his head, pulling him in deeper into the kiss. In the back of his mind, Dong knew that he should be a lot more freaked out about this, but he couldn't help but moan softly, melting into Ai's embrace. He smelled so good, he smelled like the gardens on a rainy afternoon mixed with something spicier. It caressed Dong's mind and lit a flame in his stomach, making him half-hard under his robes.

Ai's tongue licked at Dong's upper lip and with zero hesitation, Dong opened his mouth, allowing entry. Ai gripped the back of Dong's hair, exploring his mouth as all he could do was stand there and take it. And by gods, did he want to take it.

In one swift motion, Ai shifted his weight forward, pressing a thigh up between Dong's legs against his now throbbing hardness. Dong whimpered, hips jerking forward, seeking friction. It had been such a long time since he'd been touched like this. He and Lihua had consummated their marriage, of course, but that had been years ago. He touched himself fairly regularly but it just wasn't the same, they didn't have the type of relationship that some married couples had, full of passion.

Dong let his head tilt back, letting out a moan as Ai's hands wandered down his torso and back to grab at his ass. The Emperor's lips made their way down Dong's jaw and peppered their way down his neck until he reached a pulse point and began to suck.

"Hnngg." Dong whimpered, his hips now rocking at a semi-regular pace against the hot thigh between his legs. He would be more embarrassed if it weren't for Ai's cock pressing into his own hip with need. It turned him on even more somehow to realize that Ai was just as turned on by this as he was.

"Oh, fuck." Dong whispered as, far too quickly, he began to feel that pressure building in the pit of his stomach. As his breath hitched, he wrapped his arms around the other man, holding onto his shoulders from behind for purchase. "Ai..."

The Emperor stopped sucking on his throat and licked a path up to Dong's ear, nibbling on his earlobe. "Close?" His tone was teasing and heady as if he knew exactly how close Dong was and wanted nothing more than to push him over that edge.

"Ahh... yes..." Dong felt his balls tighten up. "I'm so close..."

Again Ai's lips traced the shell of Dong's ear and he whispered. "Good. I want to feel you cum against me."

That was the final straw, Dong moaned out loud as he tipped over the edge, humping Ai's thigh through it all. It had been quite some time and Dong was so turned on that his orgasm hit him in waves, another spurt of semen shooting out with each shudder. Fuck, there was so much; Dong could feel his load dripping down his shaft, as against all odds, he was still incredibly hard.

Dong came down from his high, panting and clutching Ai's shoulders. "Fuck."

With a chuckle, Ai captured his lips again. "I've been thinking about that ever since I saw you in the library yesterday." Then as if to punctuate his words, Ai pressed his hips forward, pressing his erection into the other man's hip. "So sexy."

Dong let his hands release the broad shoulders and looked around quickly to ensure that nobody was around before dropping to his knees. Ai's gaze was dark with lust, biting his lip as he realized what Dong was planning to do. Untying the front of the Emperor's robes, Dong slipped his hands underneath the fabric, pushing it to the side. He licked his lips hungrily when he saw it, angry, red, and weeping; Ai's dick was thick and Dong wanted it in his mouth right now.

It had been such a long time since Dong had given head that he reassured himself that the butterflies in his stomach were completely natural. For a moment, it seemed as though Ai noticed his nerves, but before Ai could say anything, Dong licked a stripe up his cock from base to tip, sucking lightly on the head.

"Oh, shit." Ai cursed, his hips jerking slightly.

Pleased with that reaction, Dong began taking more and more into his mouth. It had been some time since he'd last had a cock in his mouth, but he groaned headily as he remembered exactly how much he loved it. He ran his hands up and down the back of Ai's thighs, pulling shivers out of the Emperor. His hips stuttered in an aborted fashion as Ai put in heroic levels of effort not to fuck into Dong's mouth, but Dong was having absolutely none of that. He reached to the side, took one of the Emperor's hands, and snaked it through his hair, hoping that Ai would understand what he was telling him to do.

When Dong stopped moving his head, instead looking up at Ai and tightening his grip on the back of his thighs, a moment of clarity crossed the Emperor's face.

"Fuck." Ai whispered as he gave in to his urges and started thrusting into Dong's mouth. Dong gagged softly as Ai's cock hit the back of his throat over and over again and tears were beginning to well up in his eyes, it was so fucking good.

Dong gripped his own dick and using the leftover cum as lubricant, began stroking himself at the same punishing pace Ai was fucking into his mouth. He moaned, sending vibrations up the other man's length and eliciting a groan of pleasure. His hand was flying over his cock and he was so close but not quite close enough to cum. Tears painted his cheeks and his hips jerked desperately in time with his strokes. Then, finally, Ai's hips began to lose rhythm and Dong watched as Ai closed his eyes, biting his lip and came down Dong's throat. The first taste of semen was enough to push Dong over that ever elusive edge and his whole body shuddered as he swallowed, shooting onto the marble floors.

4

Chapter Four

The entire way back to his quarters Dong felt like he was floating. Did any of that really happen? Did the Emperor of China seriously just let him hump his leg like a dog and then fuck this throat like an absolute champion?

Well, if the discomfort of his jaw was any indicator, then yes, yes he did. Dong slid the door to his bedroom shut and slid down to the floor, holding his burning red face in his hands.

After they'd both finished, Ai had helped him up and planted another kiss on him before looking him right in the eyes and saying, "That was fun, we should do it again." He'd nodded and Ai had smiled at him before promising that he'd save Dong from the bores of politics after all his Emperor-specific meetings tomorrow and sending him on his merry way. Of all the things Dong predicted might come of his trip to the capital, fucking the Emperor wasn't one of them.

Well... technically he hadn't fucked the Emperor...

Was that what he had planned for tomorrow to "save him from the bores of politics"? Dong's face felt like it was on fire, he needed to calm down, he didn't know anything for sure and it would be horribly embarrassing if he showed up ready to get dicked down only for the Emperor to sit him down for tea or something.

Gods he was a horny monster.

Dong sighed and got up off the floor resigning himself to just take a bath and go to bed. The room he had been assigned to was part of a larger complex shaped as a square around a joint hot spring for guests of the palace to bathe and relax. Pulling off his clothing, he gathered up the towel hanging for him near the rear exit to his room and made his way out to the baths. Luckily they were mostly empty, Dong supposed that a majority of the officials were out in the city getting dinner together and catching up.

He folded up the towel and placed it on top of his head, stepping into the springs. He felt his muscles relaxing in the hot water and let himself sink into the springs, water coming up over his lips leaving only his nose and eyes exposed. He'd always known that he was attracted to men growing up and had even experimented with his friends in his formative years, but that had all stopped when he married Lihua. It wasn't that he thought she would have minded, but a part of him wanted to give their marriage an actual, honest chance.

Eventually, they'd just settled into the friendly relationship that they had now and he'd gotten busy with the political duties that came with his new station. It had been a while and it wasn't until he'd seen Ai in the library that he realized how much he'd missed it. Being intimate with someone and feeling his heart flutter.

Dong closed his eyes and pulled the towel off his head long enough to dunk his head in the water before replacing it. He pushed water out of his eyes with his hands and settled back down, sitting on a ledge near the edge.

Taking the time to look around, Dong mused to himself how much Lihua would like it here. It was gorgeous and close enough to the city that they would have easy access to some of China's best and most well stocked markets. Maybe Lihua could do what she'd always wanted to do and open a clothing shop in the bazaar, selling her designs to noble lords and ladies. Dong closed his eyes and grinned to himself, soaking up the relaxing properties of the spring. That would be nice; he would have to remind himself to take a trip to the markets to purchase some nice cloth for her before he went back.

After a little soaking, Dong finished up his bath and went back to his room to prepare for bed. Unfortunately, his stomach had other plans; in all the hurried chaos of the afternoon, he'd forgotten to eat dinner. After pulling on his clothes, Dong ventured out into the evening.

Surprisingly, as he walked down the street away from the palace and towards the city, there were actually quite a few people up and about. It was incredibly different from his hometown, where evenings were typically sleepy and low key, here the city streets were still bustling with life. Groups of men stumbling drunkenly from bar to bar, women walking arm in arm from one shop to another, cooing over the newest accessories, and even some children wandering the streets with their parents.

After a little bit of wandering, Dong managed to find a hole in the wall place that looked like something that he might find back home. He was excited to try new things and explore the city but after the day he'd had, he was looking for a few creature comforts. As he settled into the seat at the bar, he began to look over the menu, ordering a rice based liquor and chicken dish that he recognized.

"If I didn't know any better, I'd think you were following me." Dong looked up in surprise as a familiar silhouette sat down next to him.

"Ai?" Dong whispered, looking around to see if anyone else had spotted the Emperor. "What are you doing here?"

"What?" Ai turned his head, smirking. Dong felt the Emperor's eyes rake over him and his face began to heat up. "A man can't visit his favorite bar?"

"Well." Dong responded incredulously. "I mean, when that man is the Emperor of China, you think he'd be a little bit less cavalier about venturing out into the city alone."

Ai grinned. "I'm not alone, I'm here with you."

Dong raised his eyebrow in question, looking around again, eyes falling upon several serious looking men, sitting near the doorway.

"Okay. You got me." Ai took a drink from his own cup that had materialized in front of him as Dong had been distracted. "I brought some guards, but that's only because I wanted to eat here tonight. You being here just happened to be a happy accident."

Dong made a pleased noise of affirmation, his food arriving on the counter. "What a coincidence."

Ai leaned in, his lips brushing the shell of Dong's ear and Dong froze, food halfway to his mouth. "Now that I've run into you, though, I must say; I hope you don't have any plans for the rest of the night after this."

Dong felt a shiver travel down his spine, the implication weighed heavily in his mind. Ai's hand found its way to Dong's thigh and he could feel the Emperor's breath on his neck.

"You know." Ai continued teasingly. "I couldn't stop thinking about your mouth on my cock."

Ai's hand wandered up Dong's thigh and stopped dangerously close to his crotch, which was very quickly becoming a problem. Granted, it looked like Ai's guards had cleared out the bar leaving only the two of them, but they were still in public. Dong felt his face burn with embarrassment as Ai brushed the back of his hand over his growing erection.

Dong swallowed headily and shifted in his seat. "Is that so?"

"Yes." Ai smiled, pulling back slightly and leaning one of his elbows on the table, leaving his hand on Dong's thigh, giving it a squeeze. "How long are you in town?"

Dong sighed both in disappointment and relief as Ai removed his hand, instead turning his attention to the food being presented in front of him.

"Well, the meetings are going to continue through the week. Then after that, I was hoping to spend a few days exploring the city while I wait for my friend to finish up his talks at the university." Dong tried to turn his attention over to his meal and will his boner away by talking about Yang.

"Oh?" Ai inquired, taking a bite of his dinner.

"Yes." Dong followed suit, bringing a spoonful of his food up to his mouth. "My friend Yang is participating in some talks at the university, he's a scholar from my province. We actually traveled here together."

"And how are you enjoying the capital?" Ai asked, looking him up and down coyly.

Dong cursed at himself as he felt his cock twitch at how hungrily Ai was looking at him and continued to eat.

"I haven't really gotten a chance to see much of it honestly. I arrived yesterday and immediately found the library, then I spent the rest of the night reading. This is actually the first time I've been out in town."

Ai hummed appreciatively, licking his lips to catch some stray rice that had escaped his mouth. Dong watched hungrily, like the horrible, horny monster that he was, wondering what those lips would feel like on him.

Damn... it had been way too long since he'd had a dick in him. Adjusting in his seat again, Dong poured himself a shot of liquor and took it down in one swallow. This man was going to be the death of him.

There was no way that he didn't know what he was doing.

Dong swallowed, pouring himself another shot, he was going to need to be much less sober for this.

"Is it bad that I don't intend for you to see any of the town or its highlights tonight?" Ai asked innocently and Dong gave up, putting down his cup and turning to face the Emperor.

"Are you *trying* to get me hard in public?" He asked exasperatedly.

"Depends." Ai put down his own glass and looked up at Dong with hungry eyes. "Is it working?"

In a moment of bravery and tipsiness, Dong took Ai's hand and placed it in his lap, his cock twitching, and leaned in until their lips were inches apart. "I don't know, you tell me."

Dong could have been having a hallucination due to the lack of blood going to his brain, but he thought that in that moment he heard Ai whisper, *fuck*, taking a shaky breath in.

"Xiong." Ai turned to the guard closest to the entrance. "Get the carriage." Then turning back to Dong, he licked his lips. "We're leaving."

The second that the carriage doors closed Ai was on him, his tongue exploring his mouth and his hands grabbing anything within reach. Dong was so overtaken by the heat of the moment that he didn't even register a second thought before he swung his leg over Ai's lap, straddling him and grinding down into his erection. Ai moaned loudly, grinding his hips up into Dong's ass; Ai's hands sunk down until they were gripping his thighs so painfully that Dong was sure he would be bruised tomorrow.

Good, he thought. There was something incredibly hot about the idea of Ai's fingerprints marked on his skin, maybe they'd even last for several days.

The carriage started to move and as the road began to slant upwards towards the palace, Dong was pressed even more into Ai's chest. As they kissed, Dong ground his hips down into the Emperor's lap, feeling himself begin to leak.

Ai growled under his breath and started kissing and sucking his way down Dong's jaw all the way to his neck. Just as he reached Dong's shoulder, he bit down, hard and Dong almost came right then and there. He gasped, throwing his head back, pressing his hips forward so his hard length was pressed up against Ai's torso, trapped between them. Then if it was even possible for him to get sexier, Ai let go and dragged his tongue across the indentations in his shoulder.

Feeling blissed out without even having finished yet, Dong leaned forward claiming Ai's lips again. He only barely registered when Ai began pulling their robes out of the way and taking them both in his hand.

"Fuck." Dong whined. "Won't we have to walk back to your... ah... place?"

"No." Ai responded, whispering against Dong's neck as he held their cocks together. "They are dropping us off right at my quarters. I can make a mess of you and nobody else will know."

Dong nodded, the sly smile in Ai's voice was reassurance enough. As soon as he leaned in, kissing the Emperor again, he moaned, thrusting his hips forward a little. Ai started jerking them off together at an absolutely punishing pace.

"Fuck... you're gonna make me..." Dong whined, not wanting to shoot off too early before they even got back to the emperor's quarters. But as if reading his mind, Ai chuckled and replied.

"Good. I'm gonna see how many times tonight I can get you to cum."

"Oh, fuck..." Dong felt a wave of heat rush through him, his stomach tightening up. Ai ran a thumb over the heads of their cocks and squeezed a little tighter, getting right back to it. Dong bounced slightly on Ai's lap, humping up into the hand circling them both, getting that traction both from the hand stroking them and Ai's hardness right next to his own.

"Ahh... Ai..." Dong whined, dropping his head on the Emperor's shoulder. He was teetering on the edge, about to finish, but wanted Ai to come as well. "Come with me, Ai."

The Emperor groaned and the second that Dong felt Ai's cock pulse next to his own, it was over. He spilled his seed alongside him, thrusting up into Ai's grip, fingers digging into the Emperor's back.

They both sat in stillness for a moment panting and trying to catch their breaths, until Ai took Dong's face in his clean hand, gripping at his neck.

"I'm going to absolutely destroy you tonight."

Feeling himself already getting hard again, he lifted his gaze and smirked, watching Ai with lust filled eyes.

"Promise?"

5

Chapter Five

The second the door to the bedroom closed, robes were already being torn off and hitting the floor. Ai claimed his mouth in a kiss and backed them up towards the bed with ease, stopping when Dong's knees hit the bed and pushing him back into the plush pillows and silken sheets. Before Dong could protest about the rough treatment, not that he would, Ai was on top of him, biting and licking his way up Dong's torso.

He tore at Dong's robes, pulling them away from his skin, and immediately began covering him in bites and marks instead. Dong whimpered as Ai made his way up his chest and latched onto his nipple, grinding his hips into Dong's. Dong reached down and took Ai's face in his hands, pulling him off his chest and up to his mouth, kissing him deeply.

It was a collision of teeth and tongue, rough and sensual. Dong ran his hands up and down Ai's back and sides, even tracing down his V-line, teasing near his erection but never quite touching it. Ai growled into his neck, pulling him close and biting into the sensitive flesh underneath his ear. Dong had never had anyone be this rough with him before and he fucking loved it.

"Please." He begged, thrusting his hips up for contact.

"Please what?" Ai murmured into his ear, licking up the side.

Dong felt his eyes roll back as Ai gripped his cock, holding his hips still by straddling his thighs. "Fuck... please... fuck me."

Dong could feel Ai smile next to him, this was clearly what he'd been waiting for. "How can I refuse when you ask so nicely?"

Ai swallowed a moan as he kissed Dong again deeply. Then far too quickly, he was gone, trailing down to the edge of the bed and tossing his underwear on the floor. Ai reached his fingers up touching Dong's lips.

"Suck." He demanded and Dong was more than happy to comply. He took Ai's fingers into his mouth, sucking them like they were the most delicious thing he'd ever tasted, even taking them back into his throat like he was sucking cock. None of this went unnoticed by the Emperor, he watched hungrily before pulling his fingers back out and tracing them down towards Dong's hips. Dong almost expected Ai to tease him, going slowly and drawing it out, antagonizing him; so he was pleasantly surprised when he took Dong into his mouth to the hilt, sucking the life out of him.

He was so distracted by the pleasure that hit him that he almost didn't notice the fingers playing at his entrance.

Almost.

When the first finger sunk in, Dong felt his abs tense up. Sometimes when he was feeling particularly horny, he would finger himself while he masturbated, but he had forgotten how incredible it felt to have someone else inside him. Moaning loudly, Dong arched his back slightly off the bed, overwhelmed by the dual sensations. The drag of Ai's finger inside of him mixed with the hot, wet feeling of his mouth on his dick was the final straw. His orgasm hit him like a ton of bricks, arching his back even further he opened his mouth in a silent scream.

Only when he came back down did he think about the fact that he hadn't warned Ai even a little bit, but when he looked down all he was greeted with was that devilish smile. The Emperor used his thumb to wipe the side of his mouth, licking the cum clean off.

"That's two."

Dong could have died happy right then. But it didn't seem like Ai was even close to being done with him. Peppering kisses down Dong's inner thighs, Ai took the opportunity to add another finger, scissoring them and stretching him. He was very clearly experienced and knew exactly how to properly stretch someone to prep them. That might have bothered other people, but not Dong. No, he just ground back into Ai's fingers, gripping the sheets and holding on for dear life.

Clearly searching for something, Ai flipped his hand and began rubbing all over inside of him. Dong knew what he was looking for but had only managed to find it himself a handful of times.

"Yes." He whispered, biting his lip. Ai smirked, making a couple more moves until Dong seized up, driving his shoulders into the mattress.

"There it is." Ai cooed. While rubbing that spot over and over again, Ai expertly inserted a third finger, expanding on the stretch while distracting Dong by playing with his prostate.

Against all odds, Dong felt himself beginning to harden again. He panted, tears gathering at the corners of his eyes, threatening to spill over. Then suddenly he was empty; he whined at the feeling, his hole clenching around nothing. But then he felt it, the blunt head of the Emperor's cock pressing against his entrance.

Ai leaned forward, brushing Dong's hair out of his face. "Let me know if it's too much."

Then he began pushing in.

It had been a long time, but Ai had prepped him expertly and Dong didn't feel anything other than full and satisfied. When Ai finally bottomed out, he paused for a moment, claiming Dong's mouth again in a fevered kiss and giving Dong a chance to adjust to the thick cock seated inside him.

It was a sweet gesture but it only took a few moments before Dong began rocking back onto Ai's hips. "Please, move."

A satisfied groan fell from Ai's lips as he nodded and pulled out halfway. Then with no warning, he thrust forward, ramming the head of his cock against Dong's prostate. Everything else was a blur from that point, Ai's hips pistoned at an unforgiving speed, his grip bruising Dong's hips.

Then in a movement expertly executed, he tossed Dong's legs over his shoulders, effectively folding him in half and Dong moaned loudly. This new position not only brushed his prostate with every thrust as the other had, but was also reaching depths of him that he'd never felt before. Never in his life had he ever felt so completely full and well fucked.

"Ai... yes... yes, more... fuck..." Dong chanted a mix of garbled words resembling pleading as he felt his orgasm building again but it being his third one that night, the penetration alone was not quite enough to bring him to the edge. Blindly, Dong reached between them and took his weeping cock in his hand, stroking it madly, tossing his head from side to side. It was fast, it was dirty, and it was so fucking good.

"I'm gonna... ahh..." Dong moaned.

"Shit..." Ai cursed under his breath as Dong came, clamping down around his length. Then suddenly he was coming too, Dong's ass milking him for everything he had in him. He kept thrusting in until he stopped shuddering and collapsed on top of Dong, both of them boneless.

After a couple of minutes, Dong regained his ability for cognitive thought and sighed happily, feeling thoroughly fucked out. Ai seemed to come back into himself not too long after and groaned as he slipped out of Dong, propping himself up on his hands on either side of Dong's torso.

For a moment their eyes met and Dong thought he saw an emotion he didn't recognize flash over Ai's face, but it was gone as quickly as it had come. The Emperor sighed and rolled off to the side with a groan, leaving Dong to stare up at the ceiling.

"We should bathe." Dong turned his head and propped up on his elbows, watching Ai at the end of the bed.

"I guess we should." Dong sat up, wincing slightly at the pain in his ass.

"You alright?" Ai called back as he headed to the bathroom.

"Yeah." Dong replied, standing and limping slightly after Ai to the baths. "It's just been a while."

Ai barked a laugh and smiled back at him. "Yeah, that will do it, won't it?"

Dong made an affirmative noise of acknowledgment and dipped his toe into the already drawn bathwater. "Must be nice, having a personal hot spring."

"It is." Ai stepped further into the water, sinking down to his chest. "One of the perks of being Emperor I guess."

Dong chuckled. "There seem to be quite a few of those, I won't lie to you."

Ai shrugged and dunked his head, coming back up, hair dripping. Dong swallowed a passing intrusive thought scurried through his mind. He knew that the Emperor was sexy but for a moment he'd forgotten how beautiful he was. Averting his gaze, Dong worked on getting clean, spending special attention on his ass for obvious reasons.

"You said it's been a while." Dong looked up, curious where Ai was going with the conversation. "You don't have a lover at home?"

Dong hummed, shaking his head and pouring water into his hair. "I mean, I have a wife if that's what you're asking."

"It's not." Ai replied, a smile in his voice. "For someone who so clearly likes dick, I'm surprised that you don't have a man outside of your marriage."

Dong flushed and sunk down into the water to his nose, contemplating his answer. "I was trying to give my marriage a shot." He finally landed on this response, sitting back against the wall. Then when Ai didn't interject he continued. "My wife and I are friends, but we don't really... um." Dong shrugged, thinking about Lihua. "I was giving us a chance but by the time it became apparent that our relationship would never be like the one I was trying to let it be, I was just extremely busy with work."

Ai hummed in acknowledgment, running his hands through his hair. "Well, if you find yourself in need of any fun while you're here." Ai flashed Dong his sly grin. "My door is always open. Well, metaphorically, realistically you'll need to send a message through Mei Lan."

Dong practically choked at that. "And say what? Excuse me but can you please let the Emperor know that I have a hole or two that require filling? I think the fuck not."

Ai's laughter echoed throughout the chamber and for a moment Dong was surprised, not having heard the Emperor's genuine laugh before. His gaze flicked up to see Ai doubled over in laughter, clutching his stomach. Dong swallowed, his stomach flipping at the sight. Ai tucked his wet hair behind his ear and took a deep breath as he finally regained control.

"Damn. I knew you were hot, but I never expected you to be funny."

Dong pursed his lips. "You know, I'd be offended if I could find the energy, but given that you've just dicked me down within an inch of my life, I think I'll let this one slide."

Ai chuckled again, wiping a tear from his eye before getting out of the bath and pulling on a robe. "Here." Dong stood up out of the bath and reached his hand out to accept the robe that Ai was holding out for him.

As he wrapped himself in the robe, Ai meandered back into the bedroom.

"I will send Mei Lan with your clothes once they've been cleaned tomorrow."

Dong felt his heart drop a little, but he recovered quickly. Of course, Ai wouldn't want him to stay, he was just a fuck. Dong bit his lip and nodded.

"Sounds good. I will see you around I guess."

"Oh, and Dong." Dong turned back around and glanced over his shoulder at the Emperor. "If you want to come back for more fun tomorrow night, just find Mei Lan after your meetings and tell her 'the Emperor wanted to show me the garden', she'll know what it means."

Dong nodded and slid his shoes back on. "I will. Thanks."

Ai nodded, giving him one last smile before turning and climbing into bed. Dong took this as his cue to leave and exited the room, closing the door softly behind him.

As he walked back to his quarters, he let himself think about everything that had happened in the past 24 hours. The path was clear and the moon was high overhead, reflecting in the water from the garden, lighting up his path.

He could do casual, he was only here for a week anyway. Might as well get as much out of this experience as he could, right? Then when he got back to his province maybe he could find a consistent lover and fit them into his life. He highly doubted that he would be able to go from having mind-blowing sex every day back to no sex at all on a regular basis, and he wasn't about to force Lihua to do anything she didn't want to.

He finally arrived back at his room and sighed as he shut the door. He was feeling incredibly satisfied and a little bit sore, but there was something a little bit off that he couldn't put a finger on. But he had to get up early the next day, so ultimately he just crawled into his bed and pulled the covers up over him.

Unconsciously, Dong pulled the robe up over his nose and took a deep breath. It really did smell like him...

Nope, that was not a healthy train of thought. So instead, Dong just turned over and drifted off to sleep, leaving that problem for another day.

6

Chapter Six

The next day was absolute hell on earth. Not only was he still incredibly sore from the night before, but he was walking with a slight limp, that of course Governor Li pointed out.

"You doing alright there?"

"Ah yes." Dong stuttered, coming up with an excuse. "I tripped on my way back from the baths last night."

Luckily, he'd been alone when he bathed the night before... well, the first time anyway, and nobody had been around to corroborate or disprove his story. By the end of breakfast, Dong already knew that this was going to be a horribly long day.

On top of the soreness and everyone checking in on him to see how his "ankle" was, Emperor Ai would not stop giving him sex eyes across the table. He tried to ignore it but when he wasn't looking in that direction, he could feel Ai's eyes on him like a predator stalking prey. Then when he would finally look over, Ai would shoot him a sly smile or wink. Truthfully, Dong would have loved nothing more than to indulge in the

Emperor's flirting, but every time he decided to flirt back, his attention would be grabbed by another politician, overall leaving him with an incredibly confusing boner throughout the duration of the meal.

He was granted some relief when the groups split up by provinces, grouping the closest provinces with each other. Given that his province was considerably far away from the capital, he was given a momentary reprieve from the Emperor's succubus gaze.

Even so, once the talks were finished and the group reconvened for dinner, Dong found his heart sinking slightly as Ai was nowhere to be seen.

"Will the Emperor not be joining us for dinner?" Dong asked, leaning over to Governor Li.

"No." The Governor shook his head. "The Emperor is entertaining dignitaries tonight for dinner."

"Oh." Dong sat back into his seat, chewing on the side of his lip. He'd considered Ai's advances to be an annoyance earlier, but as the day continued on he found himself missing them more and more. Glancing up around the room, he subconsciously found Mei Lan standing near one of the exits. Immediately, he felt his face go red and he looked down at his lap.

There was no way that he was seriously considering going up to Mei Lan and having her bring him to the Emperor's quarters for sex. That was way too weird.

Wasn't it?

Dong glanced back over out of the side of his eye. They already had a code worked out so it didn't seem like this was something that she hadn't done before. That was equal parts comforting and disturbing. On one hand, she was a professional, and if this was a long standing agreement that she had with the Emperor, she would know how to handle it. However, the thought of Ai entertaining other people in his bed made his stomach turn.

He contemplated the pros and cons for the rest of dinner, remaining mostly silent but responding when spoken to and brushing off his lack of interaction to his ankle hurting him. However, by the end of dinner, he'd made a decision.

"I'm going to retire for the night." He announced to Governor Li and the other politicians he'd been conversing with throughout the evening. As he said his goodnights, the men all wished him a swift recovery from his pain and offered several remedies that they swore by, but soon enough, Dong was free.

Forcing himself to walk at a reasonable pace, he made his way over to the doorway where Mei Lan was standing. When he finally arrived, she turned her attention to him and waited.

Well fuck, she was really going to make him say it wasn't she?

"I uh..." Dong stumbled with his words, feeling his cheeks heat up a little in embarrassment. "The Emperor... um... wanted to show me the-the gardens."

Honestly, he wasn't sure what he expected, but frankly, it wasn't her bow and blank expression. "Follow me."

Dong stared for a moment as Mei Lan started off down the hallway before finally getting it together and following. He recognized the route from last night when he'd walked back, it was a little different in the light, but he still remembered. Mei Lan led him back to the Emperor's quarters and opened the doors, letting him in.

"The Emperor is still at dinner, but I will inform him of your presence."

Dong blushed. "Wait, he's not even here?" Fuck. Now he was just going to sit in Ai's room for gods knows how long for him to get back and rail him? "I um... I can come back."

Dong made a move to leave but Mei Lan side stepped so that she was between him and the door. With a sigh she said, "The Emperor told me that you might react this way upon finding out that he won't be here until later, but he asked me to assure you that it's no bother at all. He would not have extended the invitation if he did not want you here."

That gave Dong some pause, sure it was a little embarrassing but Mei Lan was right, he wouldn't be here if the Emperor hadn't invited him and it wasn't really Ai's fault that his Emperor duties were running longer than he anticipated. Dong chewed his bottom lip and looked around the space, his eyes finally landing back on Mei Lan and he realized that she was waiting for him to answer.

"Oh... okay. I will stay." Dong stepped back a few paces for good measure and smiled slightly. This seemed acceptable to Mei Lan as she nodded and then turned and left, closing the door behind her without another word.

Dong swallowed and sat down on the bed. Now that he had time, he really gave himself a chance to look around the room. He'd been a bit busy upon arrival last night so he didn't really get a genuine chance to take in the surroundings.

The furniture was all beautifully carved wood with golden accents throughout. There were a considerable number of tapestries and pieces of artwork hanging on the walls, most of them looked pretty old. Dong supposed they were likely here before Ai's time as Emperor and he'd probably just inherited the room from the previous emperor as it was.

Though, Dong thought, there were probably a couple of things around the room that were Ai's specifically. If only he could tell which ones they were.

Dong rubbed his eyes and yawned, suddenly incredibly tired. It was almost as if after sitting down on the plush bed, the events of the past couple of days had hit him all at once. Looking around again, Dong watched as the sun dipped below the roof of the palace across the court-yard. If Ai was going to be at dinner for a while, there was no harm in him just resting his eyes for a bit, right?

Dong kicked off his shoes and lay down over the covers, making himself comfortable. He would just take a short nap and when Ai got back he would wake him up and they could get right to it. Dong yawned again, this bed was unfairly comfortable. He closed his eyes for just a moment and took a deep breath, relaxing into the bed and before he knew it, he was asleep.

There was a warmth on him, lips on his neck, a hand running through his hair. Dong tilted his head back to give the phantom lips better access, humming in appreciation. As the haze of sleep cleared a little, he registered another hand on his hip, gently caressing him through his robe. It felt amazing, but not good enough.

Moaning softly, Dong shifted his hips; his body had known what was going on before he did, his cock straining against the restricting fabric.

"Mmm... Ai." Dong reached up blindly to where the lips had last been and pulled the face he found down to his own, kissing those lips gently. He was almost hesitant to wake up completely because if this was a dream, he didn't want it to ever end. But as he continued to shift awake, the sensations kept getting more and more vivid instead of fading away.

Sensually, he flicked his tongue out, kissing into Ai's mouth and sucking on his lower lip. Ai groaned but the pace remained slow and tortuous. Slowly, he let his hands migrate down to Ai's waist before pulling him on top of him. Ai chuckled lowly but went with it. In fact, as soon as Ai got his purchase in the new position, he placed his hands on Dong's chest and started gyrating his hips like an absolute gods be damned professional.

Their erections rubbed against each other with each pass of Ai's hips and finally, Dong allowed himself to open his eyes. Ai looked down at him with hooded eyes, that predatory gaze that had been torturing him all day, back in an instant.

"Fuck." Dong cursed, anchoring his hands on Ai's hips, gently encouraging the movement. "Been staring at me all day with those fucking eyes. Do you feel what you do to me? It's unfair."

Dong rolled his hips up in emphasis, pulling a stuttered breath from the Emperor. Honestly, he had no idea where all this confidence had come from, but frankly, he was just going to attribute it to his grogginess from having just been asleep. Ai's thrusts began to get more desperate and Dong suddenly couldn't take it anymore. He pulled their robes aside, freeing their lengths, and wrapped a hand around the both of them.

Ai moaned and leaned forward, claiming Dong's lips again, changing his hip motions from circular to fluid thrusts into Dong's hand. They broke apart, foreheads touching as they panted, Dong stroking them faster and faster.

"Shit... I'm so close." Ai was the first one to break the silence. "I come in and see you laying in my bed, ready for me. So sexy."

Dong felt his orgasm building in his stomach and he bit his lip to prevent a desperate moan from escaping. Ai leaned to the side barely and whispered in Dong's ear.

"I- ah... I don't think I've ever gotten hard so quickly."

"Fuck." Dong cursed, his back arching. More than anything, Ai's words had gotten to him. He felt his balls tighten up and immediately shot onto his stomach, he worked himself through the throws of his orgasm before releasing his cock and focusing exclusively on Ai. He pulled Ai's head back down, kissing and sucking at his neck as he continued to jack him off. After a couple more moments, Ai tensed and shuddered, shooting his load.

As he had done himself, Dong continued to work Ai until he was finished. Then in a huff, Ai tossed his leg back over Dong and collapsed onto his back next to him.

"Fuck that was good." Ai chuckled, turning his gaze over to Dong. Dong looked back and couldn't help it when a smile found itself on his lips.

"Yeah." Dong laughed. "It really was."

"Admittedly," Ai started, turning to his side and propping his head up on his hand. "Not what I initially had in mind when I heard that you'd used the code phrase."

"No?" Dong teased.

"Nah." Ai's grin was contagious, Dong couldn't help but feel happy when the Emperor was watching him. "I guess I'll just have to show you tomorrow night."

Dong's stomach did a flip, Ai was planning on having him back tomorrow. He was so excited that he almost forgot that he had plans to go into town tomorrow after the meetings.

"It will have to be later." Dong replied, shrugging when Ai's eyebrows quirked. "I have to run into town tomorrow evening, I have a couple of things that I promised Lihua I would grab from the city center."

Ai pursed his lips in contemplation and made a small noise of acknowledgment. "I mean." He started. "I could stand to go to town tomorrow."

Dong couldn't help himself, he turned his head back in surprise. "You want to come with me?"

"Why not?" Ai grinned and Dong felt himself immediately melt. "It will be fun, I haven't had a chance to go out in the city a whole lot since being crowned, and purchasing from local vendors will be good for the economy. Frankly, if I didn't support my people's business endeavors, what kind of leader would I be?"

"What kind of leader indeed." Dong scoffed, turning his gaze back up to the ceiling. A comfortable silence settled between them until Ai spoke again.

"Lihua, she's your wife?"

Dong turned his head back towards the Emperor to find him watching him with a curious gaze.

"Yes." Dong turned onto his side so he was mirroring Ai's posture. "We got married a couple of years ago, she was a friend of the family so it just made sense. She's a very kind and talented woman, she makes all of our clothes, in fact. That's part of why I'm heading into town, to purchase some fabrics to bring home. You know, things you can only get in the capital."

Ai hummed. "You speak very highly of her."

"Well." Dong shrugged. "It's sort of difficult to not have some sort of friendship and admiration with the person you're married to, isn't it?"

When Ai didn't respond, Dong tilted his head in question. "What about the Empress? Now that I think about it, I haven't seen her around much. Or... at all really."

A sort of pained look flashed across Ai's features for a moment before he flopped back onto his back. "Yes well, she doesn't like me very much."

Dong raised his eyebrows, "I'm sorry, I didn't mean to pry."

Ai waved his hand in dismissal. "No, it's alright. I'm the one who brought up wives." Ai sighed and started fiddling with his fingers, eyes staring directly at the ceiling. "We got married without ever meeting first, all I knew about her was what the council told me about her position in society and that she would be an advantageous match. I was doing my best to please them, so I signed the marriage order right away, she arrived two days later, and we got married.

It wasn't until after the wedding when a man showed up at the gates of the palace asking if it was too late that I realized I'd fucked up."

Dong held his breath, slowly realizing what had happened.

"I let her see him because, of course, and only then did I get the back story. They had been together for years and wanted to get married, had I taken the time to talk to her or her family, I would have known."

Ai shook his head and closed his eyes. "It was my fault, but I never would have broken them up if I'd known. He visits her once a month, but I can tell in her eyes that it's not enough."

Dong wanted to reach out and comfort Ai, his hand twitched at his side, itching to place his hand on Ai's cheek and stroke it. But he wasn't sure if it would be appreciated, so he held back.

"Anyway," he sighed opening his eyes and turning his gaze back to Dong. "She has her own quarters on the other side of the palace and I'm so busy during the day that we never really see each other."

Dong quirked up the side of his mouth and tumbled back onto his back as well. "Well, now that I know you don't have a wife coming back to share this bed with you, I'm tempted to stay. It's truly criminal that you have all this space to yourself." Dong teased.

"I mean." Ai's voice was quiet, completely different from the commanding tone he usually took. "You could, if you wanted."

Dong turned his head, meeting Ai's gaze. "Yeah?" He smiled and that seemed to pull Ai out of whatever quietness had gotten a hold of him in the last couple minutes. "Maybe I will."

Ai smiled and blew some air out of his nose in a laugh. "Well good. You're right, this bed is far too big for one person."

Dong shook his head with a smile and then moved to get up.

"What are you doing?" Ai asked, a look of confusion on his face.

"Snuffing the candles," Dong replied, incredulous at the question.

Ai just laughed and shook his head. "You don't have to do that, watch." Ai reached over to the bedside table and rang a bell. Within a couple of moments, the doors were opened and a handful of servants entered the room.

Embarrassed, Dong covered himself up with his robes and stared over at Ai as the servants shuffled around the room, systematically snuffing out the candles and drawing the blinds.

"I could have done that you know." Dong huffed playfully.

"Yes, I know," Ai answered, tugging Dong back towards him by the waist. "But then you'd have to get up, and admittedly I like you in my bed more."

Dong felt his face flush as Ai pulled them both under the covers, pulling their robes off and tossing them to the floor. Dong watched as one of the servants picked up the discarded clothes and followed the rest of the group out the door as they finished their duties. The door closed and Dong turned to Ai, his features just barely visible in the darkness.

"You're horribly spoiled aren't you?" Dong teased.

"I'm the Emperor, raised in a palace. Of course, I am." Dong chuckled and snuggled down into the bed.

"Well, at least I'm reaping the benefits of that."

7

Chapter Seven

As Dong woke, he felt like he was floating on a cloud. He had never woken up feeling so comfortable in his entire life. He stretched, feeling his skin rub against the silky sheets, and grinned to himself.

An arm wrapped around his waist and pulled him in until he was flush with Ai, chests pressing together and legs intertwined. He didn't even need to open his eyes before Ai's lips were on his, giving him sleepy morning kisses. His tired brain registered that they'd never kissed like this before, their kisses up to this point had been fueled by a fiery need and a sense of urgency, but he wasn't awake enough to take that train of thought anywhere else.

Ai's tongue poked at his lips and he opened his mouth, allowing access. He let his hand drift down to Ai's hip, pulling them even closer and in this new position he could feel that while they'd just woken up, the Emperor was sporting a chub. Groaning into Ai's mouth, he felt his own cock begin to fill.

"Morning," Ai murmured between kisses. Dong made a happy noise of affirmation, pressing his hips forward a little more.

"What time is it?" Dong asked.

"Probably mid-morning."

Dong's eyes flew open and he jerked back, sitting up straight in bed.

"Mid-morning?!" Dong tossed the covers off himself and started a mad search for his clothes. "Shit, Governor Li is gonna kill me."

Ai watched him with an amused look as he frantically flit around the room, searching for anything to put on.

"Your clothes aren't here." Ai offered, grinning his standard sly smile. "The servants took them for cleaning last night."

Dong turned around and stared incredulously with his hands on his hips. "You think this is funny don't you?"

Ai licked his lips in an attempt to stop smiling but ultimately failed. "I mean, a little."

Dong shook his head. "I am supposed to be attending every meeting this week and if it's the time that you say it is, I'm horrendously late. And if- I'm glad you think this is so amusing."

Dong crossed his arms over his chest as Ai's shoulders began to shake with laughter.

"I'm sorry." Ai wheezed between laughs. "It's just really hard to take you seriously with you standing there yelling with your dick out."

"Then help me find some clothes!" Dong threw his arms down exasperatedly and stormed over to the bedside table, picked up the bell, and rang it. Within seconds a slew of servants came filing into the bedroom and only at this point did Dong remember that he was completely naked and stared up at the ceiling, his hands in front of his crotch.

Ai at this point was rolling with laughter in the bed next to him. He was laughing so hard that he actually had tears streaming down his cheeks.

"Um." Dong started, finding the courage to side-eye the group of servants. "I need my clothes."

"Of course." The lady who looked like she was in charge spoke up, sending another girl off with a twitch of her head. "Wait here and someone will bring you a change of clothes."

Then with that, the group left, shutting the door behind them. Dong sat on the edge of the bed in a huff and dropped his head in his hands, ready to scold Ai again when he felt a hand on his wrist.

Ai pulled him down and cupped his face in his free hand. The tears had stopped but he still stopped to chuckle every now and then. "Don't worry, honestly."

Before Dong could protest, Ai shook his head and swept his thumb across Dong's cheek. It was such a sweet, gentle gesture it took Dong by surprise and even looked like Ai was caught off guard as well.

"I'll just send you with my seal, tell them that I had a meeting with you this morning. Nobody will question it, I'm the Emperor."

Too soon, Ai let go and laid back on the pillows, intertwining his fingers behind his head. Dong could still feel the place on his face where Ai had touched him, but it felt different than the way Ai had touched him before.

He was already late, he would have to unpack that later. Dong took a deep breath and rubbed his face with his hands.

"Alright. You're right." Dong turned his head as he heard the door open. A servant came in with some of the clothes he had packed for the journey and it didn't take long for him to realize she'd gone back to his quarters to grab them. He thanked her as she placed them on a dresser and got up as soon as she was gone.

"I'm just nervous." Dong admitted as he put on the robe. "I've known Governor Li for a long time and I don't want to disappoint him. This is my first big event in my position and I know that he expects a lot out of me."

"I'm sure you'll do fine." Ai replied, shifting so he was sitting up in the bed. "Besides, most of politics is getting as close as you can to the most powerful person you can and I think you've already surpassed everyone's expectations in that department."

Dong snorted in laughter, Ai was teasing him but surprisingly his words actually did make him feel lighter. He finished throwing on his clothes and turned one final time to give Ai a smile. "Thanks. I will see you later."

Just as Ai had predicted, while the other governors were a little miffed at his late arrival, the second he produced the Emperor's seal, all was forgotten and he even had a couple of people pull him aside, asking for tips on how to get a private audience with the Emperor. He couldn't really tell them the truth, so he just shrugged and suggested they try to find a common interest, like he had. Which wasn't technically a lie, but he wasn't about to tell a room full of his colleagues that the common interest they had was dick.

The rest of the day passed by pretty quickly and without a hitch. In fact, ever since it became clear that he had the Emperor's favor, Dong felt like the others were paying attention to what he had to say more and more. Even if he wasn't well informed on an issue, the rest of the group would still want his opinion.

Toward the end of the day, Dong felt a presence at his back and turned to find Mei Lan, waiting patiently for him to notice her.

Once she had his attention, she leaned down and spoke lowly so that only he could hear her. "His Majesty wanted me to relay to you that after your final meeting today, you should meet him at the back entrance near his quarters."

Dong nodded, "Thank you."

After Mei Lan retreated, he re-immersed himself in the conversation, doing his best to ignore the incredulous looks he was getting from some of the other politicians. It wasn't a secret that Mei Lan was one of the Emperor's servants and while they might not have registered him going with her yesterday, now that it was common knowledge that he had the Emperor's favor, they certainly were noticing now.

As the meeting wrapped up, Dong said his goodbyes and ducked out of the room as discreetly as he could. Stepping out into the garden path, he took a breath of fresh air; he just wasn't used to having so many eyes on him at one time, this was certainly going to take some getting used to.

The grounds were mostly quiet as Dong made his way back towards the Emperor's quarters, encountering fewer and fewer people the further back he made it, until he turned the corner, his goal in sight. At the end of the path, leaning on the wall and reading a book, was Ai. Dong couldn't help but smile to himself, the sight of Ai waiting for him sent butterflies through his stomach. He knew that whatever this was that they had was temporary and exclusively about sex, but there wasn't any harm in admitting that he had a little crush, right?

"Reading anything interesting?" Dong piped up as he made his way over. Ai looked up and smiled warmly at Dong, closing the book gently and handing it to one of his guards.

"No, it's horribly boring actually, you arriving just saved me from dying a horribly slow death from boredom."

Dong laughed and stopped just short of where the Emperor stood. He would have loved to embrace him and give him a kiss after the long day he had, but he could control himself. So he didn't.

"What is the carriage doing here?" Dong gestured over to the horses and buggy waiting for them.

Ai opened his mouth like he was going to respond but then it dawned on Dong what the Emperor was planning to do.

"Oh, no." He grinned, taking Ai's wrist and pulling him down the road on foot. "We are walking, I've already had enough people staring at me today, I don't need it happening in town too."

"But-" Ai looked back at the carriage as they passed, but wasn't truly giving any major resistance.

"You're the one who wanted to come with me. We are doing this my way today." Dong heard some chuckling from behind them and as he turned to investigate, he saw one of Ai's guards, smiling and biting his lip as if trying not to laugh anymore. Ai frowned and threw a look back at the guard.

"Well, I'm glad you find this so funny Bolin, but it's going to be you rubbing my feet later when they hurt from all the walking."

"Apologies sire." Bolin replied, looking not even a little bit sorry. Dong recognized him as one of the guards that had been with them at the restaurant when they'd first run into each other in the city.

"Have you been Ai- I mean the Emperor's guard long Bolin?"

"You could say that." Bolin managed, composing himself.

"Bolin has been my guard since I was a child."

Immediately intrigued, Dong slowed his pace and turned around so he was walking backwards. "Is that so?"

Ai grumbled, "You don't have to sound so interested."

Bolin laughed again and Dong grinned, "Does that mean you have embarrassing stories of him from when he was a kid?"

Ai whipped around and pointed a finger at the guard. "Don't you dare."

"Of course I do, I just won't be telling them as he is the Emperor and could have my head."

Dong pouted but this seemed to placate Ai who had resumed walking, every once in a while shooting a warning look at Bolin.

"That doesn't mean that I won't tell you why I was laughing earlier."

"Traitor!" Ai called out exasperatedly.

"The Emperor hasn't walked to town in almost 10 years, or really anywhere long distance for that matter."

Ai made a face that looked dangerously close to a pout and said. "It's not really my fault, my mother told me that walking was unbecoming for a prince despite my protests."

"Well it's a good thing you're not a prince anymore, isn't it?" Dong quipped back.

Bolin chuckled again from behind them as they continued their journey to the city center.

All in all, it didn't take that long to walk from the palace to the city, Dong frequently walked longer distances when he was at home. But Ai, not accustomed to the cardio was ready to sit down when they finally arrived. However, unfortunately for him, there was shopping to be done.

They browsed together for a couple of hours, picking out the fabric Lihua had requested to make them some more clothes before taking a break at one of the tea houses. Despite an invitation, Bolin decided to sit at the table directly behind them instead of with them so he could keep an eye out.

"That's pretty much everything she asked for, but I want to get her something nice. She packed me a lunch for the ride here and it saved me from going hungry or having to eat whatever unfortunate road snack that Yang brought."

Ai hummed affirmatively, taking a sip of tea. "What about that fan that you saw back at the first fabric stall? That was beautiful."

"It was." Dong admitted. "But it was a little bit too expensive for what I was looking to spend." He shrugged. "I still need money for food and necessities for the rest of the week before returning home."

Ai put down his cup and shook his head. "Let's just go get the fan, you can eat with me for the rest of the week."

Dong lifted his gaze in surprise, the warm cup heavy in his hands. "Really?"

If Dong didn't know any better, he would have thought that the Emperor was being sheepish after his offer was extended. "Yes really, I enjoy your company and I am the Emperor of China, I have more money than you could ever offer me, so just- I will consider your companionship payment enough."

Dong brought the cup up to his lips, taking a sip to buy him some time, as he was truly speechless. He felt his cheeks heat up and he swallowed, setting his cup down and blaming the heat on the temperature of the tea, even though he knew better.

"Thank you." Dong smiled softly to himself, playing with the rim of the cup. "I um, I enjoy your company as well."

Ai sighed and waved his hand, in a clear need for a subject change, Ai shifted in his seat. "So how are you enjoying the book?"

It took Dong a moment to realize what he was talking about. "Oh! I love it, it's truly unlike anything I've ever read before. I'm almost done with it, so I should be able to give it back to you soon."

Ai just shook his head and replied, "Keep it as long as you like, you're still here for four more days right?"

Dong nodded and smiled. Again he felt his heart jump in his chest, he almost had half a mind to ask if Ai was feeling the same thing but he didn't want to risk losing the Emperor's company for the next few days before he had to go back. So instead, he just finished his tea and tilted his head.

"Are you ready to go get the fan then?"

Ai's face warmed up and his posture got more comfortable as he realized that Dong was accepting his offer. "Yes, let's."

—

Now that it was later, the sun had set and lanterns were being lit in the street to shed light on the increased volume of shoppers and patrons of the restaurants and bars lining the streets. Dong and Ai walked in comfortable silence with Bolin following a couple of paces behind.

If he pretended, Dong could almost imagine that this was a date. Walking together through the marketplace, every now and then their hands would brush or someone would walk by and they would be placed in closer quarters than they had been before.

He knew that he shouldn't entertain his fantasies, but he couldn't help it. They'd purchased the fan and migrated over to the river bank to take a seat on one of the benches out of the way of the hustle and bustle. Peeking over to his side, he blushed as Ai caught his gaze, he hadn't expected him to be looking back.

Dong folded his hands in his lap and played with his lower lip between his teeth. He wasn't sure why he felt like he'd been caught doing something he wasn't supposed to, they'd done significantly more intimate and embarrassing things in the bedroom. But for some reason, getting caught looking in this romantic setting, felt different.

"Dong." Ai's voice called gently from his side. Dong felt his cheeks heat up further but did not move a muscle, so he was surprised when Ai's hand suddenly appeared in his field of vision, covering his own. "Look at me."

It wasn't a demand, nor was it a question. It was just more of a hopeful request and Dong's heart jumped at the sound of the Emperor's voice. He couldn't help himself, so he turned his head and met Ai's gaze, and right there, in his eyes was the look he'd caught on Ai's face a couple of times over the past couple of days. The one that almost reflected his own.

Dong licked his lips, his eyes flicking down to Ai's mouth. He wanted to kiss him, for no other reason than kissing him. He wanted to go back to the palace and hold him in his arms, peppering kisses all over his body, cupping his face in his hands, and telling him exactly how beautiful he was. As he locked eyes with Ai again, the Emperor's grip on his hands shifted, pulling him in closer.

Their noses brushed and Dong's breaths were coming out in stuttered puffs. Ai ran his fingers through Dong's hair, sending shivers down his spine and then finally, finally, their lips met.

8

Chapter Eight

Ai tasted like the fruity liquor they'd sampled earlier mixed with something earthier and more familiar. There was no urgency to this kiss, no pent up desire to rip each other's clothes off as there had been in the carriage ride back to the palace that one night they'd met in town by coincidence. Dong traced Ai's jawline with his thumb and sighed, relaxing further into the kiss.

Ai gently traced his tongue over the line of Dong's lips and slipped inside, exploring slowly and sensually. Dong felt his throat constricting slightly as tears gathered at the corners of his eyes and threatened to spill over. Never had he been kissed with such reverence and gentle care before in his life. He brought his other hand up to Ai's neck and held him closer, putting everything he couldn't possibly say into the kiss and just hoped that Ai understood.

A couple of tears escaped his eyes, carving paths down his cheeks but he couldn't bring himself to care. Finally, they broke apart, resting their foreheads against each other; they sat that way for quite some time before Ai pulled back and wiped the tears from Dong's cheeks.

"Let's head back." Ai smiled softly, running his fingers through Dong's hair. Silently Dong nodded and without another word, they got up and began their trek back. In direct contrast to their trip from the palace, they didn't speak, but not once did Ai let go of his hand.

As if sensing the change in mood, Bolin kept his pace slower than he had on the way to the city earlier, giving them space, disappearing entirely as they arrived at Ai's quarters in the palace.

Ai pushed the door open and softly kissed Dong's neck as soon as they stepped into the space. The door slid closed and Dong's eyes drifted shut, his hands tracing Ai's silhouette, tilting his head to allow Ai better room to pepper his neck with kisses. As they stumbled over to the bed, they didn't even bother taking off their robes, instead just opening them so they could have skin on skin as easily as possible.

Given the hardness pressed up against Dong's thigh that was growing with each moment, it was clear where this was headed, but unlike every other time they'd had sex, this was slow, almost loving. Dong took Ai by the chin and lead his lips up to his own, away from his neck, and claimed them as his own. Dong felt the side of the bed hit his knees and climbed backwards onto the mattress without relinquishing the kiss.

Ai, eager to follow, climbed on top of him, lips finally parting from Dong's so he could press kisses down Dong's body, starting with his neck, then traveling to his collarbone, down his chest and stomach, and finally landing on his hip. Dong's breathing was ragged and deep as he watched the Emperor look up at him with hooded eyes. Ai took Dong's cock in his hand and sucked lightly on the tip.

Dong threw his head back and cried out softly. Encouraged by the noises he was making, Ai took more of it into his mouth, hollowing his cheeks and sucking as he gripped Dong's thighs. Dong shuddered and arched his back before Ai pulled off and continued his journey down, sucking at his balls and then finally finding his destination, biting at Dong's ass cheeks before licking a stripe over his hole.

Dong had never had anyone do this for him before but he couldn't imagine going the rest of his life without it again. He shifted his hips slightly, precum dripping from his cock onto his stomach.

"Ai..." Dong moaned and one of Ai's hands disappeared from his thigh. Ai hummed into him, pressing his tongue past the ring of muscle, and as Dong looked up, he almost came right then and there as he saw Ai's hand moving between his own legs.

Dong whined and arched his back. "Please... Ai... I need you."

"Fuck." Ai cursed, sticking one of his fingers into his mouth before pulling it out with a pop. He shifted forward again, sucking at the head of Dong's length again as Dong felt his finger press into his ass. He keened and began rocking his hips forward, both chasing the wet heat of Ai's mouth and fucking himself back on the finger inside of him.

Dong felt like he was losing his mind completely, his abs clenching as he tried to stay away from the edge. Just as he felt like he was about to lose it, Ai pulled his head off his cock and added another finger to his ass, scissoring his fingers to loosen him up. Dong screwed his eyes shut and reached down, taking a handful of Ai's beautiful, long hair.

"Please..." He begged and by the look in the Emperor's eyes, he knew that the man had reached his limit. Ai just nodded and Dong squirmed a little at the sudden emptiness as Ai pulled his fingers out. However, he wasn't left empty for long, as he felt Ai's cockhead press up against his entrance. Pulling Ai down into a kiss, Dong relaxed as much as he could, allowing Ai to push in bit by bit.

They hadn't done as much prep as they otherwise would have so Ai went slow, checking in on Dong every second of the way and peppering kisses over his neck and face, and showering him with little compliments.

"You're doing so well."

"Taking my cock so good."

"So beautiful..."

Before he knew it, Ai was fully sheathed inside of him and Dong was gripping Ai's shoulders and holding on for dear life. Ai pulled back, looking down at Dong with a small smile on his lips before leaning in and claiming Dong's lips again. As they kissed, Ai began rocking his hips, dragging his cock in and out.

Dong let his hands wander, caressing Ai's sides and squeezing his biceps. Ai moaned into his mouth and moved his lips down, latching onto his neck and sucking. They moved together slowly and sensually, in no rush to finish as they had in the past. Just enjoying being with one another.

But soon enough, Ai's rocking became more and more hurried, stuttering at each thrust. Dong was just about to reach between them and stroke himself to the rhythm of the thrusts when he felt Ai's hand wrap around him instead.

"Cum for me." Ai murmured into his ear, and that was more than enough to push Dong over the edge, his core tightening as he came.

"Ai…" Dong called out the Emperor's name as he worked through his orgasm and that seemed to be the final straw for the other man. Dong could feel Ai pulsing inside him as he filled him up, holding him tight to his chest.

Once they had both worked through the final waves of their orgasms, they just lay there holding onto each other. They were sweaty and covered in cum but Dong couldn't bring himself to care even a little. He nuzzled into Ai's neck and placed a few kisses on the Emperor's pulse point, relishing the shivers he elicited from the powerful man.

"We should probably bathe." Dong murmured after several minutes of just laying there.

Ai made a hum of affirmation and pulled back, standing up and stretching, his softening cock hanging heavy between his legs. The sight was almost enough to stir Dong into arousal again but as he shifted, he felt something slide out of him and he grimaced. He wasn't sure he wanted to make the trip back to his own quarters to bathe, but luckily he didn't have to worry about that for more than just a fleeting moment.

"Come on." Ai held out a hand, using his head to indicate that they were going to be heading to his private baths together. Dong smiled and took Ai's hand, pulling himself to his feet, and followed the Emperor to the hot water without letting go of his hand.

Ai kissed him gently as they stripped out of the open robes they still had on, letting them drop to the floor. The pair made their way to the private baths and Dong slid into the water with a satisfied groan. The heat of the water felt so good on his aching muscles and he was eternally grateful that he hadn't had to walk back to his quarters. He'd had them walk to the city to make a point but it was a rather long trek and he was tired.

Sinking down into the water, Dong didn't expect Ai to approach him from behind, wrapping his arms around his torso. This wasn't something they did, even the one night that he'd slept over in the Emperor's quarters, they hadn't been affectionate after the fact. But now, Ai buried his face in the crook of Dong's neck and held him close, hands working their way over his body in a sensual but not inherently sexual way. Slowly he turned in Ai's hold and pressed their chests together, taking initiative and bumping his forehead against Ai's.

With their noses almost touching, Dong sighed.

"Ai..." He wanted to bring up the fact that he was going to be leaving in a matter of days, that they shouldn't be doing this, but he couldn't bring himself to verbalize his concerns. Almost as if reading his thoughts, Ai stole a quick kiss.

"Don't think about it too hard." Ai whispered, claiming Dong's lips again. Dong melted into the kiss, his fingers intertwining in Ai's gorgeous, black hair.

They kissed for quite some time, for how long exactly, Dong did not know. Eventually, they broke apart long enough to clean themselves but were right back at it again before either of them could even suggest otherwise. Now they sat in the shallow end of the bath, Dong straddling Ai, arms flung around his neck. Ai held him close as Dong kissed him just under his ear, licking, and nipping at the pulse point.

Finally, Dong settled, resting his cheek on Ai's shoulder as the Emperor traced patterns over his spine. Dong wanted to take this moment and freeze it forever so that it would never have to end; unfortunately, as all things do, he knew that it would.

Dong was in a terrible mood.

The meetings had been horribly boring and unnecessarily long, and while he was here for this purpose, he'd wanted nothing more than to stay curled up with Ai in his bed and mess around all day, never having to put clothes on. What was even worse about it was the fact that everyone around him just kept reminding him that he was in fact, not there.

He understood what a huge deal it was to gain the Emperor's favor, so he couldn't blame them, but at the same time, he just wanted to be left alone. This was supposed to be a trip for him to observe and learn but somehow, he'd been dragged into the center of the action. With the Emperor's favor in his pocket, everyone wanted to know what he had to say, even when he had nothing to say at all. Then, on top of that, everyone wanted to know things about Emperor Ai that he'd learned in the days he'd been here.

However, Dong was pretty sure that they meant government secrets or ways to gain their own favor with the Emperor. Dong only had answers to one of those two things and he sure as hell didn't want to coach any of the old men in the room through a blowjob. In fact, the idea of Ai touching anyone else just made his skin crawl.

It wasn't fair, he knew that; Ai was a powerful man and technically Dong didn't have any claim over him whatsoever. That said, Dong had let himself indulge in his secret feelings for the man last night and he was finding it particularly difficult to shove those emotions back behind the walls he'd put up initially. Every time he would resolve himself to put aside how he was feeling and focus on the work, someone would bring up the Emperor or he would think about how sweetly Ai held him last night and he would get tossed right back to the starting line where he began.

Dong sighed and rubbed his eyes.

"Dong!" Boomed Governor Li as the final meeting of the day wrapped up. Li and a couple of other politicians walked up to him, smiles decorating their faces. Dong smiled back as best as he could but in his heart, he was dreading what was to come.

"We were hoping that you'd join us for dinner."

There it was. Dong wanted to act surprised, but he just couldn't bring himself to. Earlier in the week, these dinners had just been for more established members of the party, individuals who'd been governors for quite some time. Those dinners were both a time for them to talk shop and discuss things that hadn't been on the agenda that day or follow up on ongoing issues as well as a time to talk shit about the newest of the group that had shown up that year.

His father had told him many times that should he ever be invited to one of the events, to accept it as that would be the best way to gain prestige in the group.

However.

His father had not anticipated Dong fucking the Emperor of China, which he was pretty sure was a better way to gain prestige in the group. He knew that he should be honored to be invited, but he could only feel himself bubbling with irritation. He only had one more day in town and he had been hoping to spend as much time as he could with Ai before he had to go back to his province. The very thought tugged on his heartstrings and pressed on his tear ducts.

The past couple of nights, Dong had eaten dinner with Ai and slept in the Emperor's chambers. It hadn't even been a question. After *that* night, Ai had been overwhelmingly generous with his affection; kissing Dong without any expectations for it to lead anywhere, though it often did, holding him as they did simple tasks together such as bathing or standing in a hallway speaking, and even going so far to continue his verbal adorations.

Dong didn't think that he'd ever felt so simultaneously happy and broken up about anything in his entire life. He would have a need to come up to the capital a few times a year at most and even if he made the trip more often, there was no guarantee that he would be able to spend time with Ai. The man was the Emperor of China for gods' sake. He couldn't just go canceling important meetings and political negotiations every time his, whatever the fuck Dong was to him, rolled into town.

Dong let the corners of his lips quirk up in his practiced smile and had just opened his mouth to grudgingly accept the invitation when he heard a familiar voice from behind him.

"Apologies Gentlemen." Mei Lan interrupted. "Dong will have to pass on libations tonight as the Emperor has something of great importance to discuss with him."

Several of the Governor's faces fell in disappointment but they nodded and recovered quickly, wishing Dong the best of luck in his meeting.

Bless you, Mei Lan. Dong chanted in his head as he was led away from the group of older men. Though, when he made the turn to head over to Ai's chambers, Mei Lan cleared her throat and shook her head, gesturing in the direction of the gardens.

"This way please."

Dong raised his eyebrows but altered his course, following Mei Lan into the open gardens in the center of the palace. They made their way over to a more secluded area of the gardens, closer to the library where

Dong had first encountered the Emperor, and out of the greenery, Dong saw a gazebo rise up.

That, however, was not what took his breath away. Ai was sitting in a chair, fully done up in his Emperor robes, book in hand, sipping a cup of tea. As they approached, Ai took notice of their arrival and put his book and tea down, standing to greet them.

"Thank you, Mei Lan." Ai nodded at the servant as Dong ascended the gazebo steps.

Presumably, Mei Lan took off but Dong didn't get a chance to see where she went as he was immediately greeted with warm arms and a light kiss on each cheek, the nose, and then the lips.

"Hello to you, too." Dong chuckled, his spirits lifting considerably.

"You look as though a tremendous weight has been lifted off your shoulders." Ai joked, leading them both back to the table and chairs.

"Mei Lan saved me from having to go to dinner and talk shop with a bunch of Governors."

Ai made an affirmative noise and gestured for servers standing at the edges of the gazebo to bring in the first plates as they settled in.

"It's not that I don't care to spend time with them." Dong continued, holding hands with Ai across the table. "I've just been talking with them all day and I know that the only reason that they want to talk to me is that they think that I have your ear."

Ai squeezed his hand and smiled, taking a bite of the delicious looking appetizer on his plate. "You do have my ear."

Dong rolled his eyes. "I know that, but I don't want to talk politics with you. It's not very sexy pillow talk, is it?"

Ai chuckled. "That's one of the things I really like about you, Dong. Many men would have used this opportunity to try and push some sort of agenda but not you. I can't decide if that makes you sweet or stupid."

Dong's heart swooped at the confession. It made him terribly sad to think about the fact that since becoming Emperor, but also likely his entire life, Ai had to deal with having to determine everyone's intentions.

"Neither." Dong settled on, picking up a vegetable with his chopsticks and popping it in his mouth. "I just like spending time with you."

Dong watched as the Emperor's face softened and he reached over, taking Dong's hand.

"Me too."

9

Chapter Nine

They talked until the sun set and the servants had to bring out the lanterns and pretty soon the moon was peeking over the roofs of the palace, into the gardens.

"I'm almost done with the book." Dong mentioned offhandedly. "I should be finished with it by tomorrow-"

Dong trailed off, remembering exactly why he needed to be done with the book by then. There was going to be a farewell breakfast and then everyone was going to head their separate ways, back to their corresponding provinces. Dong's heart dropped a little, he didn't know when he was going to be back and over the short period of time he'd been here, he'd grown accustomed to Ai's presence and affections.

As if reading his mind, Ai stood and took his hand, guiding him out of the chair. "Come on."

Ai led them back down the walkway to his quarters, dismissing the servants as he went. The entire walk back, Ai didn't let go of Dong's hand. When the doors to the Emperor's bedroom shut, Ai pulled him into a wordless embrace. Dong could feel Ai's hands moving up and down his back in a comforting fashion and tried to ignore the tightening of his throat. Squeezing the other man back, Dong buried his face in Ai's neck and screwed his eyes shut to prevent any stray tears from falling.

It was embarrassing how affected he was by all of this; he'd only known Ai for a week, but somehow the idea of continuing his day to day life without seeing him left Dong feeling empty. He'd never felt this way before and the worst part was that he knew that Ai probably took a new lover every month. Biting his lip, he pulled back to plant a kiss on the Emperor, combing his fingers through Ai's hair. A couple of stray tears made their way down his cheeks when he closed his eyes again, leaning into the kiss.

Ai brought his hand up and cupped Dong's face, wiping the stray tears with his thumb, not saying anything. The pair slowly made their way over to the bed without ever breaking apart and laid down on the cloud-like covers.

Dong opened his mouth as Ai licked at his lips and began to kiss him harder. The pair grabbed at each other, holding on as if the other was about to slip away and Dong cursed internally as his eyes began to burn with more tears. But instead of allowing them to ruin the moment, he flipped them, straddling Ai's hips and holding his wrists down above his head. They kissed passionately and Dong made his way down, kissing at Ai's jaw, down his neck, and onto his chest.

He paused only momentarily to pull his robes off and throw them onto the floor. Then in one motion, he took Ai into his mouth, sucking at his length, but he didn't plan to stay for long. After he deemed it good enough, he popped off and situated himself over Ai with his cockhead brushing up against his entrance. It would be a bit of a tight fit without prep but they'd had sex this morning, so he was sure it would be alright.

Ai gripped Dong's hips to help steady him as Dong caught the head of Ai's cock on his rim and slowly began working himself down. The stretch burned a little but not in an unpleasant way, it made him feel alive. Bracing himself on the Emperor's chest, he finally seated himself fully on Ai's erection and he leaned forward catching Ai's lips in a kiss to distract himself as he adjusted.

Ai was more than happy to oblige to Dong's demands, kissing him passionately and grinding his hips up every now and then to give them both the friction they craved. Finally, Dong leaned back and began circling his hips. Ai's eyelids fluttered as he pursed his lips, fingers digging into Dong's hips.

Then with all his strength, Dong lifted himself up almost completely off Ai's cock before slamming back down, eliciting a pleasured moan from both of them. It felt so amazing that once Dong started, he couldn't stop; he bounced on Ai's cock like his life depended on it, whimpering when Ai's cock brushed his prostate.

Dong could feel himself getting close, but after riding the Emperor for as long as he had been, his legs were tired and he could no longer sustain the pace required to push him over the edge. His thighs shook and he let out a breath of exasperation, but his annoyance didn't last more than a moment as Ai took that moment to flip them, giving him not one moment's rest before pounding into him at a punishing pace.

Dong's moans got louder and louder until they reached a peak where he was pleading for Ai to continue, tears streaming down his face both from emotion and the pleasure of Ai hitting his prostate over and over again. He clung to Ai as they finished, one after the other, their lips meeting once more.

They didn't really talk much the rest of that evening, after taking a bath, they just curled up in bed, kissing and touching each other until they fell asleep in each other's arms.

The following morning was a sordid affair, they'd kissed and snuggled in bed until it was absolutely time for them to get up and attend the breakfast. Unlike all the other meetings throughout this week, the breakfast seemed to go by far too quickly and before he knew it, Dong was standing in front of the palace, face to face with the Emperor as Yang readied the carriage.

After placing his luggage into the carriage, Dong extended his arm, poetry book in hand.

"Here you go. I um- I finished it, as I promised."

Ai glanced down at the book and moved like he was going to take it back but stopped himself.

"Keep it." Ai smiled softly and Dong couldn't help but feel the tears burning in the corners of his eyes as he hugged the book to his chest. Dong nodded and bit his lip, he wanted to say more, do more, but Yang was calling for him. In one swift movement, Ai pulled him into his chest for a hug and whispered in his ear.

"Goodbye, Dong."

Then as quickly as he had pulled him in, he was gone, walking back towards the palace without a glance back. Dong tightened his grip on the book in his hands and turned around, walking past Yang and sitting heavily in the carriage. As they drove away, Dong couldn't help but purse his lips, a stray tear escaping down his cheek.

Yang, being the good friend that he was, knew that something was wrong, but didn't push it, instead losing himself in his manuscripts. Dong promised himself that he would give himself time to be upset when he got back to the privacy of his own home, but for the sake of his pride, he wasn't going to cry in front of Yang. Ai had probably already moved on anyway, so there really wasn't any reason for him to feel this way, but somehow the thought of someone else in Ai's bed made everything worse. So, he decided to actively avoid that train of thought.

By the time Yang dropped him off in front of his home, it was dark out. He knew that Lihua would still be awake, however, as she knew that he would be returning tonight. Typically, he would be excited to head inside and tell her all about the trip, then watch her face light up as she unpacked the gifts he purchased for her, but he just didn't have it in him tonight. Despite all of that, however, she always tried her best for him so he would try to do the same.

Taking a breath, he stepped into the foyer and slid off his shoes. As usual, Lihua wasn't far away and upon hearing the door open, she shuffled over, giving him a warm smile.

He did his best to smile back but something about her familiar face and the comfort of home just broke down his walls and Lihua being who she was, noticed immediately.

"Dong. What's wrong?" Lihua took his luggage and placed it on the ground just inside the entryway. Gently, she held his shoulder and rubbed up and down his arm with her other hand.

"Fuck." Dong cursed under his breath as the tears he had been holding back since leaving that morning began to spill. He allowed himself to be led inside and seated at their table as Lihua put on a pot of tea. She brought him over a handkerchief and said nothing as he cried it out. Then, finally, as the tea had finished brewing, Lihua sat down across from him and poured them both cups of tea. At this point, the tears had subsided and Dong was just left feeling exhausted both from the day of travel and the intense emotions of the past week.

"What happened?" Lihua asked gently. "Is it the new job?"

Dong took the cup of tea in his hands and allowed the warmth to permeate his being, further calming him. Responding to Lihua's question, he shook his head and cleared his throat.

"No." He took a sip of the tea and placed it back down on the table. "The job is fine."

Lihua reached across the table and took Dong's hand in her own, silently prompting him to continue.

"I uh-" Dong looked up at his wife. "I don't know where to start."

Lihua shrugged. "At the beginning."

So he did. He told her everything from the moment that they met in the library to their tearful final goodbye the night before and Ai's gift to him the next morning. He spared her the particular details of their sexual exploits but explained the gist of it. He also poured his heart out to her about how he felt about Ai and how he felt his heart break when he realized he'd have to leave. Lihua was just quiet the entire time, holding his hand in hers and listening.

"I know it doesn't matter." Dong shook his head. "He will probably have someone else by the end of this week, but it mattered to me. It mattered to me a lot. And-" Dong trailed off, lifting his gaze to meet his wife's. "And now I don't know what to do."

"Well." Lihua replied, looking resolved. "The first thing that you do is stop saying that it didn't matter."

Dong furrowed his brows and opened his mouth to protest but she held up her hand.

"It clearly did matter, even if you don't think it made a lasting impact on him, which I have opinions on that I will get to, the fact that it was so impactful to you, means that it mattered."

Dong felt a stray tear drop from his eyes. "Lihua..."

"And for that matter." She continued. "I don't think that it didn't matter to him. I don't know him and I wasn't there, but from what you've told me, it seems like you became very important to him in a very short period of time. Also, you're wonderful, so if he can't see that, I don't care if he's the Emperor, he's an idiot."

Dong swallowed and pulled Lihua in for a hug. She stiffened up for a second before melting into it and patting Dong's back. They didn't really do this, but Dong really needed it and Lihua knew that.

"Thank you." He mumbled into her shoulder.

"Of course." Lihua pulled back, placing her hands on his shoulders and nodding firmly. "The next thing that you're going to do is show me what you brought back, then we will head to bed. Don't borrow tomorrow's problems for today. They will be there and you look exhausted."

Dong smiled softly and nodded in agreement. They didn't stay up very late after that, but Dong made sure to show her all the fabrics and the fan that he brought her back from the capital. He recounted the stores they'd found them at and funny moments that had occurred during their trip to town. By the time Lihua was snuffing out the candles, Dong was laying in bed, already feeling a little better. He was eternally grateful for Lihua's level head and emotional support, even if they weren't in love, he was happy to have her. His eyes closed and as he drifted to sleep, he thought about Ai and how beautiful he was.

10

Chapter Ten

Dong sat in his office, quill scratching away at the parchment in front of him, as Lihua came in with a tray of tea and snacks.

"I think it's time for a break, don't you?" Dong grinned at his wife and kissed her hand in thanks.

"Probably." Dong stretched and placed his quill back in the well. He was just about to ask what she'd brought when there was a knock at the door. Lihua wandered over to the door of his study opening to the outside and opened it up. Dong couldn't see who it was but Lihua clearly knew them. He rubbed his eyes and when he looked back up he saw Governor Li making his way over, letter in hand.

"Good morning Governor Li." Dong greeted his mentor, standing up and giving a small bow.

"Please sit Dong, I just wanted to deliver the news." Dong gestured for the older man to sit across from him and as he did, Lihua said something about getting some tea for Li as well and left quietly.

"What news?" Dong inquired, it had been pretty boring in the months since his trip to the capital. The daily duties he had going on here were nothing compared to the jam packed week of meetings from the capital and he'd since settled into a routine.

"The Emperor is doing rounds of the provinces and should arrive next week to ours."

Dong's mouth dropped open for a moment and a ringing filled his ears. He hadn't heard from Ai in three months and the first that he was hearing of him was coming from Governor Li. Dong had always assumed that the next time he would see him was when he went back to the capital, but he hadn't considered the possibility that Ai might come here. Taking a breath, he shook his head, clearing the ringing, and looked back at Governor Li.

"Sorry, I think I just hallucinated. What did you say?"

Li looked at him a little strangely but repeated the news. "Since you have his favor, the other Governors and I thought it would be best if you hosted."

Dong was at a loss for words, unable to even nod his head, but was luckily saved by Lihua as she came back into the room, placing the fresh cup of tea in front of the Governor.

"We would be happy to host the Emperor of course."

Governor Li's attention was diverted to the tea as he smiled warmly at Lihua, giving Dong a moment to collect himself.

"Yes." He got out, putting on his best practiced politician smile. "Of course."

"He won't be here long." Li took a sip of the tea. "Just a couple of days, but from what I hear, he thought it would be best to familiarize himself with the provinces. It's a little odd that the Emperor himself would make the trip, but he is young and able, so perhaps not." Governor Li shrugged and stood up, drinking the rest of the cup and setting it back down on the table.

"The tea was lovely Lihua, thank you." Lihua bowed her head and picked up the now empty cup. "But I must get going, there are a lot of things that need to get done before the Emperor arrives." Li clapped a hand onto Dong's shoulder. "Thank you for hosting, it really takes a huge weight off of my shoulders. We already know that he likes you, one less thing to worry about."

Governor Li laughed and turned to leave. Dong watched him leave but as soon as the door closed, his gaze snapped to Lihua.

"Fuck, fuck, fuck..." Dong sat back down holding his head in his hands. "No contact whatsoever for three months and now he's going to be staying at my house."

"Dong." Lihua knelt by the chair and cupped his face in her hands. "It's okay, this will be good."

"Good?" Dong asked incredulously. "I'd love to hear how this is a good thing."

"I think you just need some closure, frankly it's better that he's coming here than having you go all the way to the capital. He'll come, you will be polite and kind as I know you are and then he will leave and you can move on."

Dong watched Lihua's eyes, she was so fiery and determined, he really did love that about her. Slowly, he nodded.

"Okay." Lihua got up off the floor and walked over to the door. "I will begin preparations now. Dong?"

Dong made a small noise of acknowledgment and flicked his eyes up to his wife.

"It's gonna be okay. I promise." Then with that, she left, shutting the door softly and giving Dong a moment alone with his emotions.

It wasn't like he'd gone the three months without thinking about Ai, in fact, it was quite the opposite. He thought about him every day and it broke his heart each day that the mail came and there wasn't any word from him. Since spending the week at the palace, his sex drive had also increased significantly, but he wasn't about to force his desires onto Lihua. So, for the most part, he spent his nights fucking into his fist in the bath or even in his study, while Lihua slept in the other room.

Unfortunately there were too many people around and not enough time for him to finger himself open every time. So mostly he just came, clenching around nothing and wallowing in the ache of being empty. It quenched his immediate need but was nowhere near as satisfying as he needed it to be.

He'd thought about finding someone else, but every time he thought about it, he just ended up getting upset, thinking about Ai in bed with someone else. It was ridiculous! He was not beholden to the Emperor, he hadn't even been contacted in three months and it wasn't like Ai made any promises to him before he left. But even so, he couldn't bring himself to seek satisfaction anywhere else.

Dong leaned forward, cradling his head in his hands. Maybe he hadn't been contacted because Ai was busy, there was no guarantee that he'd moved on. Dong bit his lip and cut off that line of thought as quickly as he could.

Ai was the Emperor, if he'd wanted to contact Dong, he would have. He just had to steel himself and get through it, like Lihua had said. Maybe it would be good for him, provide closure of some sort. Dong nodded and took his quill back out of the ink, resolving to get back to work.

It was all going to be alright.

It was not all going to be alright.

The morning that Ai was supposed to arrive, Dong was so nauseous that he couldn't eat breakfast. Lihua finally convinced him to drink some tea and chew on some mint leaves for his stomach, but he just knew that if he ate anything solid, he would puke.

"This was a terrible idea." He lamented to Lihua. "I don't know why I let Governor Li volunteer me for this, it's not like he knows the extent or nature of our relationship. When you think about it, it was actually very rude of him to assume."

Dong was pacing back in forth in their living room as Lihua added some final touches to one of the new dresses she was making for herself.

"Maybe it's not too late, maybe someone else can host him and I can just pretend I caught something. Then I won't have to see him and I can miraculously recover once he leaves."

"I think it's a little late for that." Lihua replied, tying a knot at the end of the piece she was sewing. "He's still the Emperor, and..." Lihua craned her neck, looking out the window.

"And?" Dong asked, stopping in his tracks.

"I'm pretty sure they just pulled in."

It was far too late, frankly, it had been too late even before Governor Li had asked him to host. Of course, he would be the one to host the Emperor and his entourage, Dong was the only one that he knew outside of formalities from this province. Dong steeled himself and took a deep breath, he and Lihua lined up at the door in the entryway as they'd practiced and waited for their household servant to show the group in.

As the door opened, Dong felt his breath catch in his throat because standing there, in his home, was Ai. His raven black hair slid over his shoulder and hung in front of him as he entered their home. In a moment, Dong was thrown back to the library at the palace, when he'd first set eyes on Ai. His beautiful lashes casting shadows on his cheeks, the sun reflecting in his glossy hair, and his incredible cheekbones cut by the gods themselves.

He felt his jaw tense but before he could do or say anything that could be deemed unprofessional, he felt Lihua's hand on his lower back as she prompted him to bow. Following his wife's lead, he bent at the waist, keeping his eyes trained on the floor.

"Your Highness." Lihua spoke. "Welcome to our home."

They stood back up straight and Dong caught Ai's gaze, feeling his heart drop into his stomach. He didn't look particularly excited to see him, in fact, his demeanor looked a little pained.

"Welcome." Dong spoke as clearly as he could. Now that the worst had passed and he'd seen Ai for the first time, he registered the others around him. There were two guards that he did not recognize but there at Ai's side was Bolin. Dong smiled at the familiar face and nodded his head. "It's great to see you all again."

"We are honored that you've chosen to stay with us during your trip." Lihua went on, stepping back so they could enter. She had always been great at this sort of thing and for what seemed like the millionth time since arriving back home, Dong felt eternally grateful for her.

Bolin passed by and for a moment, stopped, opening his mouth like he was going to say something.

"Bolin." Ai's voice called from down the hall. "Come on."

"Yes, sir." Bolin nodded at Dong and followed the group down the hall.

Dong followed suit and pretty soon, the entire group was situated in their dining area sitting down for the lunch that Lihua had prepared.

"So." Dong tried, testing the waters. "How has your journey been so far?"

"Long." Ai replied, averting his gaze and instead focusing on the food in front of him. "It's been quite the undertaking visiting all the provinces, but I'm hoping that it will be worth it in the end."

"I'm sure it will be." Dong replied taking another sip of his tea. "After all, it must be incredibly meaningful for your subjects to see their new Emperor doing his rounds."

Ai pursed his lips for a moment before smiling. "Yes. It's been wonderful for morale."

Dong furrowed his brows slightly, Ai's smile didn't quite reach his eyes. Had he said something wrong?

The rest of the lunch was quieter, some small talk peppered in here and there until Ai finally put down his chopsticks.

"Thank you for the meal. It was delicious." He said, addressing Lihua. "If it's alright with all of you, I'm going to retire to my quarters to take a nap. It's been a long day."

"Of course." Lihua smiled softly as everyone rose from the table. "I will have Lee Lee show you to where you'll be staying." Lihua gestured to the house servant and nodded as she showed the group off to the wing of the house where they would be staying.

Again, Bolin looked as if he wanted to say something, but one look from Ai had him following along with the rest of the guards. They made their way down the hallway and as soon as they were out of sight, Dong leaned up against the counter.

"That wasn't horrible." Lihua murmured, stroking his arm.

Dong nodded but truthfully it had been. Not only had Ai actively avoided his gaze from the moment he stepped foot in their home, but he hadn't even gotten to see Ai's heartbreaking smile.

He'd really been looking forward to seeing that smile again.

"I'm going to retire to the study." Dong said, standing up straight again. "I have some work to do before we go back to entertaining our guests."

Lihua nodded and gave him an encouraging smile before turning to clear the table. Dong made his way back to the study, only letting himself take a breath once the door was shut. He closed his eyes and slid down the wall, sitting heavily on the ground. He wrapped his arms around his legs and buried his face in his knees.

Dong felt tears burning at the corners of his eyes; he hadn't let himself admit it but some part of him was hoping that upon arrival, Ai would just storm in and take him in his arms. It wasn't until that didn't happen did Dong realize how badly he had wanted that, how much he'd craved Ai's touch over the past months. Having Ai here treating him like he was just any other subject hurt far more than if Dong had never seen him again.

If they'd never crossed paths again, at least the last memory he would have would be of the day he left. The way Ai had looked at him.

Gods.

Dong sighed shakily as a couple of tears fell from his eyes and onto his robe. Then for the first time since the night he'd returned, he let himself feel the depth of heartbreak that he had been pushing down. He let it all bubble up and spill over, muffling his sobs in his sleeves until he was so cried out that he couldn't have produced more tears even if he wanted to.

He had no idea how long he had been sitting there, but he figured it was probably time to get up and resume being a human again. Dong stood and walked over to his desk, leaning forward on his palms.

He was just about to sit down when he heard a knock at the door.

"Come in." He had no idea how puffy he was from crying but it was probably Lihua bringing him tea. However, upon raising his head, he was taken aback by who he saw in the doorway.

"Bolin?" The muscled guard closed the door behind him and bowed his head. One look at Dong's face and he knew that Bolin knew exactly what he had been doing in here since disappearing from the kitchen.

"I knew it." Bolin shook his head and stepped forward a couple of paces.

"Please." Dong shook his head. "Don't mention this to Ai, I will be fine I promise-"

"You two are ridiculous." Bolin interrupted and for a moment Dong didn't know what to do, he stood there struck silent.

"Forgive me. I'm aware that I'm overstepping my bounds here and in fact, I'm going against direct orders from the Emperor but I can't just stand by."

Dong furrowed his brows, confused.

"Ai came here to see you." Bolin stated as if it was the most obvious thing in the world.

"I-" Dong shook his head. "He's just here for rounds, to meet everyone in the provinces as the new Emperor."

Bolin sighed heavily. "Come on Dong, when has an Emperor ever taken the time to travel to every province themselves?"

Dong opened and shut his mouth several times trying desperately to come up with a response, but he couldn't think of one. It was odd now that he thought about it.

"He's been miserable since you left." Dong stared at the guard unbelievingly. "He's never had a companion like you before and he'd have me beheaded for telling you this, but he's being a petulant child. He has it in his head that you're better off here, with your wife, and that he'd only be a bother by telling you how much he misses you."

"I-" Dong stuttered, his heart felt caught in his throat.

"He told me that he just wanted to see you, and that's why he started this whole venture. He wanted to know for sure if you were happier without him and if you were then he'd leave you alone. I got the feeling that you were just putting on a brave face because you felt similarly, but he's convinced that you have moved on.

He's an idiot. Anyone paying attention could have seen that the way you looked at him when he came in wasn't that of someone who's moved on."

Dong swallowed. "W-where is he?"

"His quarters."

Dong took off immediately and as Bolin stepped to the side, he heard the guard murmur something along the lines of "finally".

Dong stormed down the hall, catching sight of the guards stationed outside of Ai's room. He half expected them to stop him, but they seemed to be in the know because once he got close enough, they just stepped aside.

He'd cried far too much to cry more now, Dong was just pissed. He threw open the door and shut it behind him aggressively.

"I thought I told you not to disturb me, Bolin." Ai's voice carried from around the corner but stopped short as Ai rounded into the space. "Dong."

"You absolute ass."

11

Chapter Eleven

"You absolute ass." Dong spat, crossing his arms.

Ai recoiled as if he'd been slapped and opened his mouth to respond, but Dong was quicker.

"Bolin told me everything." Dong watched as Ai's expression changed from shock to anger to sheepishness in seconds. "How could you?"

Dong took another step into the room.

"Dong I can explain..."

"Why couldn't you have just told me you missed me?"

"He shouldn't have-"

"I didn't even get a letter from you over these past months."

"I-" Dong took another step, further closing the distance between them.

"You let me believe that you forgot about me. That you didn't care about the time we had spent together."

Dong cursed internally as he felt, against all odds, tears gathering at the corners of his eyes.

"And then you come here and expect me to, what? Go against your wishes and tell you that I've missed you every single day no matter what I do?"

Ai's expression quickly melted into disbelief, but Dong wasn't finished.

"That the night I got back, I cried to Lihua for hours and every day since then, there's been an ache in my chest that nothing can remedy no matter how much I try." Tears had begun to spill, rolling down his cheeks, burning paths into his cheeks.

"I don't go a single day without missing you like a hole in my chest and some stupid part of me hoped that you'd come today and tell me how much you missed me too. When you didn't I went into my study and cried until I couldn't breathe, you stupid fucking i-"

Before Dong could finish his sentence, Dong was enveloped in Ai's arms and lips crushed by Ai's, like he'd dreamed about over the last passing months. He couldn't help it, he melted into the touch, tears trailing down his cheeks.

"I'm sorry." Ai murmured against his mouth before claiming his lips over and over again. "I'm so sorry."

Ai stepped forward, pressing Dong's back up against the wall and gripping his cheeks in his hands, wiping away his tears with the pads of his thumbs. He kissed Dong like he was the only supply of air in the room, desperately and without abandon. Dong wrapped his arms around Ai and gripped at his robe in the back, pulling him closer, closer...

One of Ai's hands slid back, cradling the back of Dong's neck and deepening the kiss further. That was just fine with Dong, he needed all the space between them to be gone; for the first time since the day he left, Dong felt whole again. Ai kissed down his jaw and over to his neck before bringing his hand back to Dong's cheek and pressing their foreheads together so their noses were touching.

"I will never forgive myself for putting you through that." Ai whispered, gently rubbing the tip of his nose against Dong's. "I missed you, every second, from the moment you left."

"I was an idiot, I thought..." Ai's voice cracked a little. "I thought that maybe I'd taken advantage of you, that you'd just want to return back to your life here and remember everything we had as a distant memory. It was selfish, but I wanted you to tell me you wanted this and that you weren't just going along with it because I'm the Emperor.

Because it did mean something to me, Dong, it meant everything to me. I haven't ever felt this way about anyone and that scared the shit out of me. Gods, I pretended like I needed to do a tour of all the provinces just on the off chance that I'd get to see you again."

Ai laughed and Dong gripped the back of his shirt harder; he was sure that he was wrinkling the fabric but he honestly couldn't care less.

"I never want you to feel that way ever again." Ai pulled back his face from Dong's and met his gaze. "So let me tell you what I should have said to you before you left the palace. I care about you, deeply, and thinking about you finding someone else and having what we had makes me sick, so sick that I can't sleep sometimes. My bed is too empty without you in it and I know that you live here, but I need to know Dong. I need to know that you're mine."

"Yes." Dong murmured bringing their lips together again. "Yes, yes, yes... I felt the same way. You're the Emperor, there was nothing stopping you from taking another lover and getting anyone you wanted but when I thought about anyone else touching you..." He shuddered and Ai ran his fingers through his hair, placing kisses all over his face.

"You never have to worry about that. Ever." Ai dropped his hands from Dong's face and opted for wrapping his arms around his waist, pulling him close.

Dong threw his arms around Ai's neck and buried his face in the Emperor's shoulder. For the longest time, they just stood that way, holding each other, when they heard a knock at the door. Neither of them answered, but the door slid open anyway, slowly closing again.

"Thank the gods." It was Bolin, Dong lifted his gaze without letting go of Ai and gave him a little smile. "I hadn't heard from either of you and I wanted to make sure that everything was okay."

"Yeah." Dong replied, wiping the tears from his cheeks. "We are fine."

"Better than fine." Ai chimed in, kissing Dong's face and burying his own face in his neck. "But you still disobeyed direct orders." He added as a second thought, turning his attention back to Bolin.

"I know and I'm sorry." Bolin bowed deeply. "But I am charged with looking after your well being and-"

"I know." Ai conceded, smiling gently. "But, I think you should probably leave now." Ai turned his gaze back to Dong, hungry and wanting.

Ai didn't wait for Bolin to respond before his lips were on Dong's again. Dong would have felt more embarrassed if he didn't hear the door open and shut one more time, indicating Bolin's exit.

Dong threaded his fingers through Ai's beautiful, long hair and licked at his mouth, requesting entrance. Ai willingly leaned into the kiss further, deepening it, running his own tongue along the inside of Dong's bottom lip. Dong felt his heart hitch as Ai stepped forward again, pinning him up against the wall, this time bracing them there with a leg between his thighs.

The pressure of Ai's body against his was enough to send blood south, filling his cock. It had been too long, he'd missed Ai's body, his smell, his everything. Letting his hands roam, he traced Ai's sides until he reached the Emperor's hips; he gripped his hipbones and pulled Ai's hips forward until they were fully flush with his. Ai panted and kissed Dong deeper as their hips made contact, Dong could tell how desperately Ai wanted this too.

Ai's hardness pressed up against him and he gripped the back of Dong's neck, further deepening the kiss as he began to rock up against him. Dong let his hands slide down further, brushing Ai's ass. Dong moaned into Ai's mouth, shifting his hips against the thigh between his legs, rutting against it with his now fully hard cock.

"Ai." He murmured between kisses. "Please. Need you..."

"Yes." Ai whispered back, like a promise. He reached down between Dong's legs and cupped his aching erection; Dong's breath caught in his chest and his head fell back as he moaned loudly. Ai continued rubbing him through his clothes as he began kissing down his neck. His cock felt hot and heavy, Ai's touch was going to make him cum just from rubbing him through several layers of clothing.

"Ai- stop." Dong pleaded. "I'm going to cum if you keep- ah-" Dong couldn't stop his hips from jerking forward into Ai's touch over and over.

"Then cum." Ai murmured teasingly in his ear. "Cum for me baby."

That was it, baby- that was more than enough to tip him over the edge. Dong gripped Ai's shoulders as if his life depended on it, his knees giving out slightly as he came. He shot his load, soaking through his robes and into Ai's hand, shaking as he rode out his climax. As he came back to reality, he was hit with the overwhelming knowledge that Ai was tipping over the edge as well. At some point, he'd pulled himself out of his robes and was furiously masturbating to Dong coming in his palm.

Ai's core tensed up and he bit his lip as he painted Dong's robes with his seed. Dong kissed him through his orgasm and ran his hands through Ai's hair as he began to relax. But Ai wasn't even remotely done with him, no. Not breaking the kiss once, Ai pulled Dong back away from the wall and walked them into the center of the room where the futon was laid out. He leisurely stripped away both of their clothes and deposited them somewhere on the floor nearby.

They had both just finished but that wasn't stopping Dong from running his hands up and down Ai's naked body feverishly like he couldn't get enough. Want and desire still pumped through his veins, his ass clenched around nothing as it had most nights since he'd been back.

"Ai." Dong whimpered, biting at the shell of the Emperor's ear.

"I know baby, I have you." Ai reassured him, laying them both down on the bed. Reluctantly, Ai moved his lips from Dong's and made his way down south, between his legs. In one smooth move, Ai flipped Dong over so he was on his hands and knees, ass in the air. Dong could feel Ai's large hands kneading his ass as an animalistic growl escaped him. Dong's breath began to pick up again and his dick twitched in interest when he felt Ai's hot breath on his hole.

"Please." Dong pleaded, pressing back unconsciously into Ai. Clearly not wanting him to have to ask a second time, Ai spread Dong's ass and licked over his hole, eliciting a broken moan from the other man. He kneaded at Dong's ass cheek with one hand as he used his tongue to circle Dong's asshole, his other hand tugging gently at his balls.

Ai's mouth seemed to want to be everywhere at once, tasting all that he could of his lover. One moment, Ai was biting Dong's ass, the next his tongue was making its way over his supple thighs, then he was mouthing at Dong's balls. Finally, Ai decided exactly where he wanted to be and penetrated Dong with his tongue, thrusting it in and out.

Dong sobbed, pressing back into it.

Yes, yes, yes. Dong thought or maybe begged, he couldn't tell anymore, his cock now fully hard again and hanging heavy between his legs.

"Please Ai…" Dong begged. "I need you inside me…. Now."

"Fuck." Ai cursed, pulling back. Dong heard wet slurping noises coming from behind him but was left in the dark only a few moments longer as he felt Ai's finger circling his entrance. Seemingly as impatient as him, Ai slid his finger in to the knuckle and waited only a moment before thrusting it in and out.

"I've been dreaming of this tight ass for months baby." Ai sounded so incredibly debauched, breathing heavily, his own hardness poking at Dong's thigh as the Emperor prepared him. "I can't tell you the number of times I woke up in the middle of the night only to find myself laying in my own cum, the memory of you on my lips."

Dong groaned as Ai added a second finger, pushing back into them.

"Nobody else would do, only you. Thinking about you always makes me so hard, do you feel what you do to me, baby?"

Ai thrust his hips forward, rubbing himself up against Dong's backside. Just at that moment, Ai brushed his fingers over the sensitive ball of nerves and Dong keened, arching his back.

Ai chuckled, "I never stopped thinking about doing this again, not for one single day." Ai thrust his fingers in and out with each syllable, emphasizing each word before flipping his wrist and rubbing at Dong's prostate.

Dong shuddered, oversensitive from cumming already but desperate for more. It wasn't enough, he'd finger fucked himself a couple of times over the past months but it was a poor substitute for Ai. Dong arched his back and whined.

"Please…" Dong could feel tears pinpricking their way to the surface in the corners of his eyes. He could feel himself getting hard again and he was desperate for more stimulation; he needed that stretch, the parts of him that could only be reached when Ai fucked him. He needed it so badly that he couldn't stand it anymore. "Please fuck me…"

Ai ran his hand up and down Dong's side as he added another finger. "I will baby, be patient."

"I- ah- I've been patient." Dong retorted. "There is nothing in the world that satisfies me the way that you do Ai, I need you- please."

"Fuck." Ai cursed, clearly doing his best to exert some self-control in the situation. "Me too baby, but I don't want to hurt you, it's been a while and you're so tight. I can't wait to know how you'll feel around my cock."

Dong whined and pressed his hips back onto Ai's fingers desperately trying to help him along. Taking a little pity on him, Ai flipped him over onto his back and leaned forward taking Dong in his mouth. Had he not just cum minutes before, he was sure that he would have climaxed right then and there. Ai took him further into his mouth, and into his throat; Dong was so distracted by the pleasure that he almost missed it when Ai slipped a third finger inside.

"Yes, yes, yes!" Dong chanted, moving his hips back and forth so he was simultaneously fucking into Ai's mouth and also back on his fingers. Ai swallowed around him and Dong couldn't hold back his voice anymore, he moaned, loudly. The guards outside could definitely hear him but he couldn't bring himself to care. He had waited too long for this, it had been too long since he had been full.

Ai pulled off Dong's cock with an obscene slurp and flexed his fingers one more time before pulling those out as well. Dong whined at the sudden emptiness but was content again as Ai leaned forward, kissing him deeply.

"Are you ready?" Ai whispered against his lips.

"Yes." Dong answered with zero hesitation. "Hurry, please."

Ai continued to kiss Dong as his hand guided his cock to Dong's ass. Dong gasped lightly when he felt Ai's blunt head press against his entrance. He licked into Ai's mouth and pulled his face in closer.

They both groaned as Ai pressed in, tantalizingly slow. It was a familiar burn, the feeling of being stretched so intensely, and Dong felt his breath pick up even faster.

"Ai- yes." Dong moaned, encouraging him to sink in deeper. It took both no time at all and all the time in the world before Ai was finally, finally seated inside him, their hips connected.

"Dong... baby..." Ai groaned and Dong felt the Emperor's cock twitching inside of him. "Please, I need-"

"Yes, I need you. Please move." Dong begged, knowing exactly what he was asking. At the confirmation, Ai slid out halfway before connecting their hips again, with a roll of his own. Dong gripped desperately at Ai's shoulders and met Ai's thrusts as best he could.

Ai picked up the pace and settled into a rhythm until the only sounds that could be heard in the room were the slapping thrusts and the moans of the two men. Dong finally let the tears spill over, half out of pleasure and half out of relief. He had really thought that he would never have this again and that thought had nearly killed him. There was no way that he could ever go another day without having Ai in his life.

Ai hiked Dong's leg up onto his shoulder and adjusted the angle, causing Dong to cry out. The new angle was positioned in such a way that every thrust was hitting Dong's prostate head on. He felt himself clench around Ai's cock, pleased with the moan it tore from the Emperor's lips.

"Dong..." Ai chanted, eyes shut. "You're gonna make me cum. Fuck."

Dong could feel his orgasm building, pulling his muscles tight and drawing his balls up. "Yes, Ai, please... cum inside me."

Ai cursed under his breath as his thrusts became more desperate. This new pressure was exactly what Dong needed and he felt himself reach the point of no return.

"Yes, fuck, Ai... I'm cu-ahh." Dong's back arched as he came, untouched, all over his stomach and chest. The orgasm seemed to continue on and on as Ai's thrusts became more erratic, still hitting his prostate over and over again, until Ai shuddered, slamming his cock all the way inside Dong's ass.

Dong made a soft sound of pleasure; he could feel Ai's cock pulsing and emptying inside him.

It was everything he needed.

As soon as Ai's orgasm passed, Dong pulled his face in one more time, this time kissing him softly on the lips. Ai adjusted like he was going to pull out, but Dong stopped him.

"No, leave it in." Dong pulled Ai down fully until he was laying on top of him. Ai blew some air out of his nose in a laugh but kissed the side of Dong's neck, running his fingers through Dong's hair.

"Of course."

12

Chapter Twelve

Dong lay there, entwined with Ai for what seemed like forever. Ai just kept tracing patterns up and down Dong's back and arms, pressing his lips into Dong's hair and kissing his head every now and then.

The sunlight trickled in from between the slats in the window and illuminated the dust particles floating in the air. Dong couldn't remember the last time he'd been this relaxed; even when they had been having sex every day, they never allowed themselves to be this openly affectionate. Dong had thought that doing so would make Ai uncomfortable, but now that he knew his feelings were reciprocated, he didn't hold back.

Dong looked up at Ai, their noses almost touching.

"Hi."

"Hi." Ai smiled, gently kissing Dong's nose and then lips.

"We should probably get up and head back to the main area of the house," Dong said begrudgingly. "I'm sure that Lihua has questions and as much as I don't want to share you, you did come here for work reasons."

Ai scrunched his nose in distaste. "Well, technically, I came because I wanted to see you. But, yes I suppose you are correct. I did promise that I would visit the local governors after settling in."

"Would you say that you are adequately settled in?" Dong teased, shifting his leg between Ai's.

"I would say so." Ai smiled. "I will have to let the governors know what a great host you've been."

Dong groaned and laughed to himself. "Please don't, the last thing I need is the Governors getting any ideas about me. I still need to work with them, you know."

"Yes, yes." Ai acquiesced, lightly kissing all over Dong's face. "I know. Don't worry, your secret is safe with me."

Dong smiled and leaned in for one more kiss before moving to get up. As soon as he shifted his weight, however, he grimaced, feeling the cum starting to slide out of his ass. He looked around for any sort of towel or rag, but when he didn't see anything he sighed.

Ai watched him in confusion for a moment before chuckling and finally realizing what was happening. "One moment."

Ai hopped to his feet and wandered off into the private dressing area, coming back with a rag in his hand.

"Here, let me help."

Once they were both adequately cleaned up, Dong opened the door into the hallway, immediately blushing deeply upon seeing the two bodyguards standing out there.

"Why are you embarrassed?" Ai teased, rubbing his arms. "You knew they were there, you passed them on the way in."

"I know." Dong hissed, his gaze stuck to the floor. "It's different seeing them, I had almost forgotten and now I was just given two of China's most well trained and competent reminders that now *more* of your guard knows and has listened to us having sex."

Ai laughed. It was light and happy and almost made up for the sheer levels of embarrassment that Dong was feeling right now. This, this was the smile and laughter that he'd wanted to see when they'd first arrived.

"Try not to think too much about it, it's one of the hazards of fucking the Emperor." Ai teased as he encouraged Dong down the hallway.

They were still bickering amongst themselves when they wandered out into the living room. As they entered, Dong heard the light tinkling of Lihua's laugh coming from the kitchen. Dong gestured to Ai to follow him and together they made their way into the kitchen.

Lihua had made a pot of tea and was sitting at the table with Bolin, laughing at something that he'd said. Once again, Dong was flooded with a rush of thankfulness for his wife.

"I see you two are getting to know each other." Ai spoke up, garnering the attention of both the individuals in the kitchen. Bolin moved to stand but Ai waved him off. "I don't suppose you have any extra tea for us do you?"

"Of course." Lihua moved to stand but Dong put a hand on her shoulder.

"I'll get the cups." Dong smiled down at his wife and pressed a kiss to her cheek. Lihua raised her hand to cover Dong's and squeezed gently. Ai sat down, joining the pair as Dong walked over to the cabinets and pulled down two more cups for himself and Ai.

He set the cups down at their respective places and sat down next to Lihua, across from Ai. Lihua had already picked up the teapot and poured the pair their own cups of tea.

"So." Lihua started, putting the teapot back down. "I take it you two have worked through your miscommunication?"

"Um." Dong stuttered, feeling the blush creeping back up to his cheeks, suddenly very interested in the cup in front of him.

"Yes." Ai continued, reaching over and taking Dong's hand in one of his own. "We did."

"Good." Lihua nodded, satisfied with their responses. "Bolin was just telling me that your highness has about half of the trip left to go after this."

Ai sighed, but kept Dong's hand in his own, interlacing their fingers. "Yes, I'm sure Bolin told you the genuine reason for this trip."

Lihua's lips quirked up at the side and she moved to take a sip of her tea. "I'm sure I don't know what you mean sire. Will you please explain?"

Ai looked over to Dong for help but Dong only shook his head. This was just like Lihua, giving him a hard time because he'd made Dong so upset.

"Well." Ai started. "I missed Dong, he uh- became important to me over the week that we spent together those months ago during the con- ference and I wanted to come and see if he felt the same way."

Lihua nodded and exchanged a knowing glance with Bolin.

"I was telling Lihua that you both should come to the palace to visit once the tour is over." Dong and Ai both perked up at this possibility.

"Really?" Dong looked at his wife and smiled at her nod.

"I don't see any reason why we shouldn't." Lihua stated confidently. "Dong, you work for the government." She gestured politely at Ai. "Here is the government. If he says that we should take a visit, I don't see any reason why we shouldn't."

Ai began to laugh, it started off as a chuckle in his chest and very quickly became a full bout of laughter. When he finally caught his breath and wiped a stray tear from his eye, he looked back over at Dong.

"I see what you mean now." Ai nodded. "She is wonderful."

Despite her bravado not one moment prior, Lihua diverted her gaze and pursed her lips. Dong could swear that he could see a flush making its way up her neck.

Pretty soon he and Bolin joined in the laughter and Lihua scolded them for making fun of her, which only made them laugh harder. Dong was pretty sure that he hadn't felt this happy in a very long time.

Ai had sent a carriage to gather them once his tour was over and Lihua couldn't have been happier. They'd packed some of their belongings and hopped in the carriage to make the journey to the capital.

Lihua was exceptionally excited as she'd never been to the capital before. Dong promised her that he would show her all of the shops where he'd found the fabrics and that they would be sure to make their way to the market as soon as they could.

After Ai and his guard had left, he and Lihua had a long conversation about his relationship with the Emperor. In the end, Lihua had declared that she would be quite alright sleeping in their quarters alone if he wanted to spend his nights with Ai. After getting over the embarrassment of what his wife was implying, Dong had agreed. He cared deeply about Lihua but his whole body and soul yearned for Ai, he didn't think that he'd be able to be in the same city as him without sleeping in the same bed.

Now that they had finally communicated their feelings, it was like the dynamic had shifted overnight. Ai touched and kissed Dong any chance he got and once he left for the rest of his tour, Dong started getting letters every day. He couldn't write back because of the speed at which the Emperor and his entourage were traveling from town to town, but he kept every letter that he received preserved in a journal.

It was truly incredible how much of a difference Ai's visit had made, and as much as he appreciated the letters, he was just aching to see him again. When they crossed into the capital, he was practically vibrating with excitement, but he kept himself as composed as he could, pointing out landmarks and particular stores he'd shopped at to Lihua as they passed.

Soon enough, however, they were making their way up the hill to the palace and Dong couldn't hide his excitement any longer. He was sure that the amount he was smiling was ridiculous, but he couldn't help himself. They were so close.

Upon approach to the front of the palace, Dong didn't see anyone waiting outside to greet them, but his disappointment was short lived as the carriage didn't slow as they passed the front and continued on.

"Where are we going?" Lihua asked, watching the front of the palace pass by.

Dong smiled to himself and relaxed back into the seat a little. "They're taking us to the Emperor's personal quarters."

Lihua looked over at him with an excited look on her face. Dong smiled, he remembered the first time that he had been summoned to the Emperor's quarters. It was easy to forget exactly how rare and exciting a private audience with the Emperor was. When they met, Dong had no idea who Ai was and so their relationship developed a little differently than how most people would go about building a relationship with the Emperor.

They turned the final corner and Dong was practically vibrating. It had been several weeks since he'd last seen Ai and knowing that he was going to come to visit somehow seemed to make the days go by slower than ever. Dong swallowed and couldn't help the grin from spreading over his face as they pulled up and there waiting to receive them was Ai and Bolin. Suddenly Dong was thankful that Ai had chosen to meet them away from prying eyes because there was nothing that he wanted to do more than jump out of the carriage and kiss Ai senseless.

The carriage rolled to a stop and as soon as the door opened, Dong was on his feet and making a beeline for Ai. It only took five steps in total because Ai was rushing to meet him halfway before he was in Ai's arms again at last. Dong buried his face in Ai's neck and inhaled, letting the comforting scent wash over him, fully relaxing him at last.

"Hi." Ai whispered, holding him as closely as he possibly could, wrapping his arms around Dong's waist entirely.

"Hi." Dong pulled back slightly to grin at the Emperor and meet him in the middle for a kiss. Only after a few moments of kissing and enjoying each others' presence, did they seem to remember that they weren't alone.

Dong pulled back from the embrace, interlacing their fingers together. He wanted to check in with Bolin and Lihua but he was not willing to pull away completely from Ai.

"Thank goodness you two are here." Bolin started, grinning softly and taking Lihua's luggage. "He's been insufferable for the last couple of weeks, so excited that you are coming to stay for a while."

"Oh, I'm sure, he was equally excited to see me as he was Dong." Lihua joked and in his peripheries, he saw Ai blush, tilting his chin down bashfully.

"Miss Lihua." Bolin turned his attention back to her and gestured for her to accompany him down the walkway. "Let me show you to your quarters. We will make sure to reconvene with these two for dinner tonight."

"That sounds lovely, thank you." Lihua beamed at Bolin and turned to nod her head at Dong and Ai. "You two have fun, we will see you tonight."

They turned the corner and Ai looked back at Dong with a devilish smile.

"Come on." Ai teased, pulling Dong towards the Emperor's quarters. "Let's take advantage of the time your wife has so graciously given us."

Dong smiled ear to ear and followed Ai into the room. Evidentially the servants had been briefed ahead of time in regards to the sleeping arrangements because just as they crossed the barrier into the space, Dong caught a glance of his luggage sitting in the corner of the room on the side of the bed.

"Presumptuous of you to assume that I'm going to be staying in here." Dong teased. "Maybe Lihua wanted me to stay with her."

Ai turned around and pulled Dong in by his waist, kissing him gently on the lips. "Somehow I think she'll understand."

Dong smiled into the kiss and pulled Ai into another, and another, and another. "She may have mentioned something about that before we left."

"Oh, did she?" Ai chuckled.

"Mmmm." Dong nodded. "She did."

"Well good." Ai trailed kisses over Dong's face and down his neck before planting a gentle bite at the connection between his shoulder and throat. "Because I made sure to clear my schedule for the next couple of days and if you think you are leaving this room, you are sorely mistaken."

Dong shivered at the implication as Ai continued to pepper him with kisses and love bites. He wrapped his arms around Ai's waist and leaned into him, grasping at his robes from behind. As incredible as it was, Dong wanted to continue kissing his lover, so he made a small noise of distress and dipped down to capture Ai's lips in a passionate kiss before standing back up straight.

Dong cupped Ai's face and kissed him with everything he'd been feeling over the past few weeks. He kissed him bruisingly, pulling him as close as he could possibly manage. Dong felt his heart beginning to speed up and his breath start to come a little faster. Now that they were truly alone, it was like they couldn't keep their hands off each other.

Of course Dong was only a man and as soon as things took a turn for the hot and heavy, he felt the blood begin to rush south. But kissing Ai wasn't just about that, Dong felt fulfilled and satisfied just being near Ai. Being this close to Ai did things to him that he couldn't explain any other way than that it made him feel complete.

Dong stepped into Ai and ran his fingers through Ai's long, dark hair. He nibbled at Ai's bottom lip and relished in the noise it pulled from the Emperor. Ai leaned back into him and wrapped an arm around Dong's waist, and started moving back towards the bed. Together they tumbled over into the sheets, Dong sighed and ran his hands up and down Ai's sides, smiling as Ai nuzzled into Dong's neck, biting and kissing as he made his way down.

Dong could feel himself hardening between his legs and groaned as Ai bent his knee, rubbing his thigh up against Dong's crotch. Dong slotted his legs with Ai's, bringing their hips together, their cocks rubbing at each other through the fabric with each movement of the hips.

"Baby." Ai whispered in Dong's ear as he reached down and grabbed Dong's ass. "I'm gonna take such good care of you. Show you exactly how much I missed you."

Dong shivered and nodded. It was all he could do, as words didn't seem to be coming very easily right now as Ai's hand slid further down, fingers playing at his hole through his robe. Then with renewed franticness, Dong stripped the offending piece of clothing off of himself as quickly as he could, pulling at Ai's as well. Ai chuckled and did the same, tossing their robes to the side.

Ai hooked a leg around Dong's and used the momentum from the new position to flip them. Dong could feel himself flushing from the tip of his ears all the way across his chest. Ai pulled back and made his way down towards Dong's hips before hiking Dong's legs up, over his shoulders. Dong barely had time to register what was going on, let alone ask any questions before Ai was eating him out like he was a man starving.

Dong wailed, unencumbered, his cock already leaking precum on his stomach. As Ai's tongue circled Dong's hole a couple of times, Dong clenched the sheets and when he felt the wet heat breach him, Dong pushed his hips up hungrily.

"Please, please..." Dong pleaded. What he was asking for, he wasn't entirely sure, but all he knew was that Ai was going to give it to him. He had promised after all.

Ai gave in to Dong's wails and abandoned his post, replacing his tongue with his fingers, skipping over one and starting with two. He kissed up Dong's thighs until he reached his cock; he mouthed at the shaft, working his way up to the tip. Dong's thighs were trembling at the double stimulation by the time he pulled the tip into his mouth.

Ai swirled the head around a couple of times with his tongue, curling his fingers and pressing on Dong's prostate.

"Ai.... I'm so- fuck... I'm gonna-" But before he could warn Ai completely, he felt a firm hand grip around the base of his cock. Dong whined as his orgasm was staved off with Ai's free hand. Ai popped his mouth off of Dong's' cock and grinned devilishly.

"Can't have that can we?" He teased. "You're going to wait until I'm inside you."

Dong whimpered again, but this time it was laced with arousal and anticipation. That threat shouldn't have sounded as hot as it did, but somehow it only made him harder.

Ai slid another finger inside of him and began stretching him in earnest, his hand never leaving Dong's cock. Thankfully he had busied himself kissing all over Dong's stomach and thighs, giving him some relief from the double stimulation.

Then finally, after what seemed like an eternity, Ai pulled his fingers out.

"You ready for me baby?" Dong would have given him a harder time for making him wait, but Ai sounded completely wrecked. Dong wasn't entirely sure that he was going to last much longer either, so instead, he lifted his head and stared down into the dark expanses that were the Emperor's beautiful eyes.

"Yes. Please Ai, I need you."

"Fuck." Ai cursed, lining himself up. They both held their breath as Ai began to push in, it was almost too much. But with Ai's grip holding him around the base of his cock, he was still safe from shooting his load before Ai was ready. As soon as Ai was fully seated inside of him, Ai's lips were on his own, kissing him senseless.

Without parting their lips, Ai began thrusting his hips back and forth, slowly at first and then quickly picking up speed.

Dong felt tears begin to spill down his cheeks, he needed to cum. It felt so incredible, he was so close, but yet still so far with Ai's grip on him. He couldn't quite push over the edge.

"Please- Ai, let me... ah... let me cum." Dong begged, dragging his nails down the Emperor's back.

"Yes, yes..." Ai chanted, his hips beginning to stutter, then in an answer to all of Dong's prayers, he let go of Dong's cock and whispered. "Cum for me."

Dong's vision went white immediately and he came harder than he had ever before in his life. He barely even registered Ai groaning and stilling above him until he dropped down on top of Dong, chest heaving. Silently, Dong traced up and down Ai's spine, completely and utterly sated; they then laid there together until Dong drifted off to sleep, happier than he'd been in quite some time.

13

Chapter Thirteen

The next morning, Dong woke to the feeling of fingers combing through his hair. He shifted slightly and reached out, his arm wrapping around Ai's torso, pulling him in closer. Ai chuckled and adjusted so that their legs were intertwined and one of his arms was wrapped around Dong's back, the other resuming petting his hair.

"Good morning." Ai murmured, kissing the top of Dong's head.

"Mmmm." Dong replied sleepily. "I think we missed dinner with Lihua and Bolin last night."

Ai chuckled. "I think you are correct. Maybe we should locate them and have breakfast together to make up for it."

Dong smiled and stretched up, pressing a soft kiss to Ai's lips. "I think that's a great idea."

After a little bit more time spent cuddling and canoodling in bed, they both finally got up. Dong set off to the area of the palace Lihua was staying and Ai went looking for Bolin. As Dong walked through the palace grounds, he found himself walking slower in the garden areas. The memories he had here were worth reliving every time he had a chance and he was excited at the prospect of making more memories here with Ai.

Finally, Dong turned the corner, he would just head inside and see if Lihua was awake. If she wasn't he could wake her more gently than a knock on the door would. Quietly, Dong opened the door and stepped inside, pausing in shock as he came face to face with something he didn't think he would be seeing this morning.

Lihua was already awake and dressed.

And so was Bolin, who was holding her face gently with his giant hands and kissing her sweetly on the lips.

"Um." Dong accidentally broke the silence, causing the pair to freeze and look over at the doorway. "I can come back."

Bolin took three large steps back right away and bowed at the hip. "No need, apologies Dong. I will go and make sure the Emperor is ready for the day, goodbye."

Dong watched, an incredulous open grin growing on his face as Bolin moved as quickly as he could across the room and out the door, shutting it with as much grace as Dong was sure he could manage at the moment. Raising his eyebrows, a manic grin now spread across his face, he turned back to his wife. Lihua was staring directly at the floor, blushing from the tips of her ears to her neck.

"*Li*hua." Dong shout-whispered across the room.

"Don't." Lihua covered her face with her hands, shaking her head.

A chuckle escaped Dong's lips and he took another step forward. "Lihua." He tried at a normal volume.

This caused her to peek through one of her fingers at Dong but immediately went back into hiding the second the saw the look on his face.

"Don't *laugh* at me Dong," Despite her best efforts, Lihua's shoulders began shaking with laughter.

The moment Lihua dropped her hands to her sides and Dong caught a glimpse of her face, clearly trying not to laugh harder, he lost it. Dong bent over, clutching his stomach, laughing harder than he'd laughed in a long time. To his side he heard Lihua begin to lose her battle as well until she was laughing alongside him, unabashed and loudly.

"Lihua." Dong got out between chuckles, wiping the tears from his eyes. "If you were unsatisfied in our marriage, you could have just said so."

"Oh, shut up." Lihua smacked him lightly before sitting down on the edge of the bed to catch her breath. Dong walked over and sat down next to her, breathing deeply and regaining his grip on himself.

Once they'd both calmed down, Dong peeked over at her through his peripheries, a small grin playing at his lips.

"I was going to tell you." Lihua said, her gaze still straight forward towards the door.

Dong shook his head. "When?"

"This morning." Lihua replied. "We were just about to come get you two for breakfast, but it seems you had the same idea. I'm just thankful it was just you and not also Ai. I don't think I could survive the embarrassment."

Dong nodded before turning his head fully to look over at his wife. "Bolin? Really? He's what? Twenty years older than you?"

"Oh, says you Mr. I'm Fucking the Emperor, who is also a man."

"Touché." Dong conceded. "But really though, where did this come from?"

Lihua flushed a little but met Dong's gaze. "We connected when Ai came to visit you, then he started sending me letters." Lihua shrugged. "I like him. He's very sweet and caring."

Dong nodded. "I always got that sense from Bolin as well."

Lihua made an interested noise and Dong continued.

"He was very kind to me when I was here for the conference and the fact that he cared enough about Ai and by proxy, me to go against the Emperor's orders and tell me how Ai was feeling just tells me how much he cares."

"So." Lihua asked tentatively. "You're alright with it?"

Dong smiled softly and nodded. "Yes, I'm fine with it. You deserve happiness too, Lihua, and if Bolin is that for you, then I wouldn't even dream of standing in the way."

Lihua seemed to let out a breath before standing and extending her hand to Dong.

"Come on, I'm sure that Ai and Bolin are waiting for us."

Dong smiled wider and took her hand, standing and pulling her in for a hug. Lihua hesitated for only a moment before she chuckled, burying her face in Dong's chest, and wrapping her arms around his waist.

"I do love you. You know that right?" Dong asked, pressing a kiss into Lihua's hair.

"Yeah." Lihua replied, squeezing a little tighter. "I love you, too."

"Come on." Dong let his arms fall away and Lihua nodded, following as they made their way to the door.

Just as Dong opened the door, he met eyes with Ai, making his way down the garden pathway with a bashful looking Bolin. However, as they came closer, Bolin looked between them and seeing their smiles, let his shoulders relax a little.

"Dong." Ai called out as they crossed the threshold into the building. "It seems as though, while I was looking for Bolin, he was looking for me. I see you found Lihua."

"That I did." Dong let his gaze wander over to Bolin, giving him a warm smile. Lihua giggled a little and moved over to stand by Bolin.

"I feel like I missed something." Ai stood with his hands on his hips, looking between the three of them with an adorable crease in his brow. Dong closed the distance between them and took Ai's arm in his own.

"Come on your Royal Highness, I will explain on the way. I'm starving."

Ai looked over at Dong and relaxed into his side. Then they took off through the garden, towards the dining hall, Lihua and Bolin tailing behind them.

Dong mostly left them alone as he explained the whole situation to Ai, but he did sneak a glance or two back at the couple and smiled a little as he saw Lihua's little blush dusting her cheeks and a genuine smile playing at her lips.

As they arrived in the dining hall, breakfast had already been laid out and tea was being poured by the palace servants. In the corner of his eye, Dong saw a familiar face.

"Mei Lan!" He exclaimed, waving at the servant at the end of the table, directing the others.

Hearing her name called, stoic faced as always, Mei Lan walked over to the group and bowed deeply at the hips.

"Good Morning Emperor Ai, Dong, and guest."

"Mei Lan, you know who I am." Bolin chided as Lihua chuckled into her hand.

Mei Lan's blank gaze trailed up to Bolin and she tilted her head. "Yes, but I don't typically greet you, you are the Emperor's guard." Mei Lan pursed her lips slightly. "If I were to greet every member of the Emperor's guard I think we might be here all day."

Bolin sighed as Lihua patted his arm sympathetically. Dong turned a little to present Lihua.

"Since you already know Bolin, this is Lihua, my wife." Dong half expected a bit of a reaction out of that one, considering she was intimately familiar with the fact that he was sleeping with the Emperor, but he pouted a bit when she remained as stone-faced as always.

"Pleasure to meet you." Mei Lan bowed again, a little shallower this time, but still reverently.

"It's good to see you again Mei Lan." Dong spoke, pulling Mei Lan's attention back to him.

"Yes." Mei Lan replied. "Now, please take your seats for breakfast, the tea is at the perfect brewing temperature right now and I would hate for you all to miss out on drinking it at the perfect temperature."

Then with that, Mei Lan turned around and gestured for the servants to pull out their seats. Dong chuckled and as they sat, Lihua caught his gaze from across the table.

"Is she always like that?" Lihua whispered loudly to Dong.

"As far as I know." Dong looked over to Ai, who nodded, eager to provide additional information.

"She grew up in the palace, both of her parents are servants here as well so she's what we would consider, exceptionally well-behaved." Ai chuckled at the last phrase. "I'm sure she lets loose at some point but when that is, I have no idea."

"Please enjoy." Mei Lan piped up again before bowing along with the other servants and shepherding them out of the room.

The meal was delicious, as all meals in the palace were. Dong had learned during his time at the palace for the conference that nothing was ever done halfway here. The meals were always cooked to perfection, the tea was always the highest quality tea leaves from the province dedicated entirely to growing tea, and the garden was maintained so well that if you didn't know any better, you might think that the plants were simply suspended in time. When he had been here previously, he hadn't had a whole lot of time to simply enjoy everything that came with being in the palace.

Dong was grateful that he was given this chance, not only to be here, but given a second chance with Ai. Glancing to the side, he watched as Ai laughed and joked with Lihua and Bolin. He looked so happy, so unencumbered; this was the smile that he had wanted to see so badly when Ai had shown up at his house all those weeks ago.

"What do you think Dong?" Dong was snapped out of his thoughts and back to reality as Ai looked over in his direction.

"I'm sorry." Dong laughed, rubbing the back of his neck. "I didn't catch that."

Lihua shot him a knowing glance and he fought to make sure that the blood didn't rush to his cheeks too quickly.

"I said, that we should take a trip into town today, show Lihua all the fabric shops that you and I looked through when you were last here." Under the table, Ai reached over and squeezed Dong's hand comfortingly.

"I think that's a great idea." Dong smiled. "I'm sure that she'll be able to find plenty of hidden treasures that I missed. She has always had an eye for that sort of thing."

Ai smiled back at him and rubbed his thumb on the back of Dong's hand. For a moment, Dong just sat and watched Ai, everything else in the world melting away until it was just the two of them, hands entwined. Dong felt a sense of overwhelming calm overtake him, he could just get lost in those eyes forever.

Oh.

I love him.

It wasn't anything like the poems he'd read or the stories he'd heard. There hadn't been a sudden strike of lightning, no sudden realization like a bucket of freezing water being poured over his head, it had been slow and comfortable, like the warm water of the hot springs, trickling over him. He was pretty sure that it wasn't a sudden thing either, while this was the first moment that he was acknowledging it, it felt like he'd been here for quite some time.

Dong couldn't put his finger on when he'd fallen. When Ai had come to visit him at home? No, it was before that. Some time in the span of a week that he'd been staying here for the conference, he'd fallen in love with Ai and hadn't even noticed. Somehow, this man had made his home in his heart and declared his intent to stay.

"Come on." Bolin's voice brought him back. "Let's start towards town, the markets have been open and bustling since the wee hours of the morning."

"That's a great idea." Lihua piped up, letting Bolin take her hand and help her up.

As they made their way out of the dining hall, Ai pulled Dong aside, gently cupping his face.

"Hey, you alright?" The worry line in between Ai's eyebrows brought a smile to Dong's face. Instead of answering right away, Dong leaned in and pressed a soft, sweet kiss to Ai's lips. Pulling back, he brought a hand up to Ai's hair and ran his fingers through it.

"Yeah, I'm fine."

"Yeah?" Ai asked, still not fully convinced.

"I promise." Dong replied, bringing Ai's hand up to his lips and kissing his fingers. "I'm great."

Ai seemed to relax a little, finally believing him. "Alright, come on, let's go."

Bolin's prediction seemed to be correct, the markets were open and while there were plenty of goods to browse, most of the food stalls were erring on the side of empty.

"Restaurants need their ingredients for the day and farmers will often trade with each other in lieu of money." Bolin explained. "I'm not down here very often at that time, but you really should come see it. There's something comforting about the organized chaos of it all."

The group bobbed and weaved their way through the crowd, stopping at stalls and shops as they went. As predicted, Lihua was drawn immediately to the tailors and fabric shops, but finally not looking for anything specific, Dong allowed himself to browse. There were so many different kinds of shops that he'd never considered before; back home there was maybe one shop that sold decorative items for the home but everything else was more practical. It seemed that here in the city, luxury and excess were the standards.

Stopping in front of a bookshop, a leather bound journal caught his eye. He was running out of space in his current one and could use a new journal. Dong reached down and picked it up; it was hand bound in leather with a waterlily pattern embroidered on the front. It was also closed with a tiny silver clasp and seemed to come with a quill and ink.

"That's a beautiful journal." Dong turned to see that Ai had come up behind him and was looking at the little book over his shoulder.

"It is." Dong replied. "I have a journal that I like to write in at home but I've had it for quite some time now and I think it's probably time I get a new one."

Ai made a small noise of approval and wound his arm around Dong's waist.

"Let me buy it for you." Ai murmured into Dong's ear.

"Ai." Dong replied. "I appreciate it, but I can buy it."

"I know." Ai swiped a thumb across Dong's cheek. "But I want to buy it for you. Can't I spoil you a little?"

Dong smiled and turned the journal over in his hands. "I think you already spoil me Ai."

"That wasn't a no." Ai grinned back.

"That wasn't a no."

14

Chapter Fourteen

Dong rolled to his side, stretching out as he stirred back to consciousness. After the group had gotten back to the palace, Ai and Dong had settled down for a bit of a nap. Dong truly hadn't meant to fall asleep, since he didn't usually sleep during the day, but the day of travel followed by their trip to the markets had really taken it out of him. Stranger still, as he rolled over, he became aware that he was the only one in bed.

Pushing himself up on his elbows, Dong looked around, Ai was nowhere to be seen but the double doors leading to the gardens were open. It seemed to be a little after sunset, the lanterns were lit and it was mostly dark outside but it didn't feel too late, there was still some color painting the sky. Dong swung his legs out over the side of the bed and got up, wrapping a sheet around himself in lieu of putting clothes back on.

Ai had been so tired that he just fell on the bed and passed out immediately upon return, Dong on the other hand had taken the time to get out of his clothes from the day. Dong turned back around to see if Ai had maybe taken his clothes off at some point during their nap but instead of a full set of clothing or even nothing at all, he was greeted with the sleeve of the robe that Ai had been wearing before.

Dong picked it up, confused. It wasn't even the full sleeve of his robe, but rather the very end that hung away from his arm at the wrist. Now even more motivated to find Ai, Dong took the sleeve and started to head towards the open doors. The double doors led to a private area of the garden for the Emperor's particular use only so Dong wasn't specifically worried about any dignitaries accidentally seeing him wrapped in a sheet.

As he turned the corner into the garden, there was Ai, sitting in the gazebo, a cup of tea in his hand and a book in the other. Looking down at his arm, sure enough, part of his robe was missing. Not wanting to disturb the serene mood that surrounded Ai and the garden, Dong walked quietly down the stone path, holding up the sheet so that it wouldn't drag on the ground. As he got to the steps of the gazebo, Ai looked up from what he was reading and greeted Dong with a loving smile.

"Ah, you're awake."

"Yes." Dong replied, walking up the steps and taking the seat next to Ai at the table. Ai immediately moved to pour Dong a cup of tea and Dong started to look over the spread of snacks and desserts. "And you seem to be missing part of your sleeve."

Dong held up the piece of fabric that he'd gathered from the bed and raised an eyebrow at the Emperor. Ai looked down at his arm as if he was surprised for a moment before nodding bashfully, a smile playing at his lips.

"Ah, yes."

"Why?" Dong asked, picking up a particularly tasty looking treat.

"Well." Ai shrugged. "You were sleeping and I didn't want to wake you, but you were sleeping on my sleeve."

Dong blinked a couple of times. "So you just cut it off?"

"So I just cut it off." Ai confirmed.

Dong opened his mouth to ask what he was sure would be a multitude of follow-up questions when Ai held up his hand and shook his head.

"It's not a big deal, I have thousands of robes. But only one you, and I wanted you to get the sleep you needed."

Dong shut his mouth and just watched Ai for a moment in the moonlight. Never in his life had he ever experienced someone so loving, so caring, and so genuine.

"I love you." The words slipped from between Dong's lips before he could think any better of it and for one terrifying second, Ai said nothing back. He looked at Dong with surprise for a moment, but was then on his feet, closing the distance between them. He planted a searing kiss on Dong's lips, holding him by the back of his neck to deepen the kiss as much as he could. Too soon, Ai pulled away, but only far enough that he could speak, their noses still touching.

"I love you, too."

Dong felt his heart jump and he grabbed Ai's face bringing their lips together for another kiss. Ai kissed back feverishly and passionately, licking into Dong's mouth, their tongues tangling together. Ai's free hand made its way to his waist and in one fluid movement, Ai pulled Dong to his feet without breaking the kiss and up against him.

"I love you, I love you, I love you..." Ai chanted between kisses and Dong could feel tears rolling down from his eyes. He had waited so long to hear those words, all that time he'd been at home, wondering if the Emperor had moved on, all seemed worth it now.

Dong threaded his fingers through Ai's hair and pulled down a little to gain more leverage, taking control of the kiss. He was already naked and the second that Ai started kissing him, blood started rushing south. Dong pressed his hips up against Ai's, rubbing his erection on Ai's hip.

"Please, Ai…" Dong prayed out loud, he could feel the sheet slipping and knew that pretty soon he would be standing in the garden stark naked with a raging hard on but he couldn't bring himself to feel even the slightest bit embarrassed by it all. Ai put a hand on Dong's shoulder and began leading him down to the ground without breaking their kiss. Once they were on their knees, Ai pressed forward, shifting Dong all the way to the ground, sitting on top of the sheet that had once acted as the barrier between him and the world.

Ai moved forward even further, positioning himself between Dong's legs, pushing his knees out further.

"Touch yourself for me, baby." Ai commanded softly. Dong almost whined, his hand rushing to touch his cock. Ai watched as Dong wrapped his hand around his leaking hardness and gave it a cursory stroke. Then, as if satisfied, Ai nodded and shifted slightly, Dong was about to protest about him leaving when Ai started to untie his robe. Dong watched, stroking himself as Ai stripped down for him, throwing his robe to the side. Ai watched him hungrily, his own hand finding its way to his own cock and stroking it, using the precum from the tip to lubricate it.

Dong had to drop his hand away from himself because the vision of Ai masturbating to the sight of him was too much for him to handle, he was going to cum. As if reading his mind, Ai shook his head and placed Dong's hand back around himself.

"Cum for me while I open you up baby, I want to watch you come undone."

Despite already being so close and not wanting to come so soon, he couldn't help himself at the plea. Dong began stroking himself in earnest, his hips rocking into his hand as he watched Ai stroke himself leisurely. Ai placed a single finger in his mouth and closed his lips, pulling it out, wet, from between them and leaned forward to place a kiss on Dong's inner thigh.

The warmth between his legs made Dong's cock twitch with want and his arousal was only spurred on more as he looked between his legs and could still see Ai's arm moving below him. The fact that Ai was getting off on this was almost too much for him to handle, he was so close.

"Ai... I'm..." Dong cried. He inhaled sharply as he felt Ai's finger play at his entrance, he knew that the second Ai pushed his way in, it would be over. "Please." He begged.

The moment Ai pushed his finger in, Dong felt the tension snap, his balls drew up and he arched his back as he shot cum all over his chest. With Ai pumping his finger in and out, Dong's orgasm seemed to last forever. When he finally came down, he looked down at Ai again, his eyes were screwed shut and his breathing was rapid. Chasing his own orgasm, Ai jerked himself off for a couple more strokes until he was trembling, his arm motions considerably slower as he worked himself through it.

As he opened his eyes again, Ai pulled his finger out, Dong groaning unhappily at the sudden emptiness, but he wasn't disappointed for long. Ai took his fingers on the hand he was using to open Dong up and ran them through the cum on Dong's chest, lubing them up further. Then, if that wasn't sexy enough, Ai replaced his finger and worked in a second before lowering his lips to Dong's stomach and licking up the remaining cum.

Dong groaned as he watched his lover clean up the rest with his tongue like it was the most delicious delicacy on earth. Once he was done, Ai kissed his way up Dong's torso, still scissoring his fingers, and brought their lips together again in another kiss. This one was less fevered with desperation but still passionate, sweet, and loving.

The night air felt soothing on his naked skin as they kissed, the heat building from their contact was enough to keep them warm and there was something exciting and romantic about being this way with Ai in nature. Ai scissored his fingers, stretching Dong thoroughly, kissing him through it. Then once he was ready to take another, Ai kissed his way down Dong's jaw and over to his neck, sucking lightly on his pulse point and using his mouth as a distraction as he worked in a third. The slow pace that Ai was using to prep him wasn't something he'd ever done before but somehow that just made it so much better.

The drag of Ai's fingers moving in and out, the light kisses being peppered into his skin, and the gentle breeze moving through the garden was almost overwhelming. Dong gripped Ai's shoulders, panting. Ai was very intentionally avoiding Dong's prostate but even so, Dong felt himself hardening again between his legs, and based on Ai's heavy breathing, he didn't need to look to tell that Ai was in the same boat.

Without a word, Ai took his lips again and pulled his fingers out, wiping them on the sheets below. Cupping Dong's face, Ai took a moment to kiss him slowly, readjusting so that he was hovering over him. Dong ran his fingers up and down over Ai's sides, eliciting a tremble from the other man. Their chests grazed each other as Dong felt Ai's length bump up against his ass. Dong arched his back slightly off the ground and tilted his hips so that the head of Ai's cock was catching on his hole.

Ai's breath hitched and slowly, kissing Dong reverently the whole way, he began to push in. There was no rush, no desperate chasing to orgasm, it was only the two of them, under the moonlight, together. Unlike the other times they'd had sex, they weren't chasing pleasure exclusively, it wasn't about that and for that reason, Dong was grateful that Ai had gotten them both off before they had actually begun. This time, it was just about the two of them, connecting as closely as two people could, sharing each other on such a deep level that they could possibly express their love.

Once Ai was seated completely inside Dong, they took a moment, kissing and touching each other in every way they possibly could. Dong pulled Ai down on top of him completely instead of letting him hover; Ai was already inside of him but Dong needed to be closer, needed more, and the direct skin contact over the rest of him sated a deep need for his lover.

Ai shifted slightly and pulled his head back so he could look at Dong. Now that Dong really had a moment to look, he realized that he recognized that face Ai was making. He'd caught glimpses of it in the times they were together before he had to leave, but it had only been in short moments. Dong smiled, his chest filling with happiness, this was the first time that Ai was truly letting himself be fully vulnerable, letting Dong see how he felt. It was a precious gift, more precious than any palace, or gold, or treasure that Ai could offer him.

Dong dragged his knuckles down Ai's cheek softly and nodded, knowing that Ai would understand what he was trying to say without having to truly say anything. Ai nodded back and buried his face in Dong's shoulder, rocking his hips slowly.

The friction of Ai's cock inside of him mixed with the way that Ai was holding on to him like he was the most precious thing on earth had tears gathering at the corners of his eyes. However, unlike so many times before, he didn't fight it, he didn't try to swallow them away, he let them fall freely as they felt the need. Ai would understand, he wouldn't ask or ridicule him for being emotional, he would just kiss them away and hold him close.

Ai began kissing at the side of Dong's neck and worked an arm underneath his waist, tilting his hips down and Dong's breath hitched. This new angle had Ai brushing his prostate with every movement, it wasn't enough to push him over the edge but it felt amazing. Dong felt his breath pick up slightly as Ai continued the slow and steady rocking of his hips.

Dong brought a hand up and carded his fingers through Ai's hair, holding on to him and encouraging him to give his neck more attention. Understanding immediately, Ai opened his mouth, tracing his tongue over a spot on Dong's neck that he had been kissing the moment prior before pressing his open mouth to Dong's neck and sucking at the skin. Dong let out a pleasured moan and began rocking his own hips back to meet Ai's thrusts. The arm underneath Dong tightened and Ai began to let his whole body rock back and forth instead of just his hips.

With each movement, Dong's cock began to leak even more, now trapped between them. Dong cried out into the night, muffling himself in Ai's neck. Ai took a deep breath and then leaned back, pulling Dong onto his lap, staying seated inside of him. Understanding his role in this new position, Dong planted his feet on either side of Ai's hips and began to bounce. This new angle allowed him to sink even further down than he had been before.

Dong hooked his arms around Ai's neck and planted a messy, passionate kiss on his lips. He could feel his climax building again and he wanted to make Ai cum. He traced his tongue over Ai's lips the way he knew that he liked and began to roll his hips more sensually in more of a grind than a bounce. He knew it was working when Ai gasped, gripping his back; Dong could feel the tiny moon shaped crescents of Ai's fingernails digging into his skin.

What a perfect way to remember their night under the stars.

"Dong... if you don't- fuck I'm gonna..." Ai swore.

"I know." Dong smiled, pressing their foreheads together. "Me, too."

Ai nodded, grinding his hips up to meet Dong's and suddenly all caution was thrown to the wind, both of them were desperately chasing orgasm, panting and grabbing at each other any way they could. Then, Dong was cumming before he could prepare himself, he threw his head back and thrust jerkily. Vaguely he registered Ai gripping his hips tightly and cursing before Dong could feel Ai's cock pulse with each wave as he came inside of him.

As he came down, Dong leaned forward, kissing Ai before draping himself over his lover letting them just hold each other. As Dong closed his eyes, Ai tracing up and down his spine, he thought to himself that there was no place in the world that he'd rather be.

15

Chapter Fifteen

Dong lay there on the sheet, his head on Ai's chest as they enjoyed the silence of the night. It was just warm enough that they could lie naked in the garden, a light breeze playing at their hair. After some time, how much exactly Dong didn't know, he felt Ai shift under him and he was suddenly reminded of the poem he'd read the first day he'd arrived here all those months ago.

"In the quiet gardens," Dong recited. "The voice- like a song, penetrates my heart and calls to my soul."

"I know not," Ai continued, pulling Dong closer. "To whom it belongs. But I know now…"

"That I can never live without it." Dong finished. He nuzzled in closer to Ai who pulled him in.

"I think I understand it now." Dong continued into the night. "The feeling that the author had when writing that poem."

Ai made a small noise of acknowledgment and Dong looked up at the stars, they were so numerous and expansive, it almost made him wonder how it was possible that the two of them could have found each other in this life.

"It feels like fate." Dong continued. "That we met when we did."

Ai didn't respond but rather turned onto his side so that they were facing each other and pulled Dong into a kiss.

"I was thinking the same thing." Ai replied, running his fingers through Dong's hair. "I've never-" Ai paused as if he was contemplating exactly how to word what he was going to say next.

"I've never had someone that I've been able to trust as much as I trust you."

Dong opened and closed his mouth several times before he ultimately decided to remain quiet as he couldn't trust his own voice. He knew how much that meant to Ai, he'd only mentioned it in passing a couple of times but Dong knew that most of the people in Ai's life took advantage of the fact that he was the Emperor. He was sure it was incredibly difficult to know who was spending time around him because they actually cared and who was remaining in orbit simply because of what he could do for them.

"I love you." Dong whispered, their noses touching. "I may not be much, but I will always give you all of me."

"No." Ai replied, shaking his head softly. "You are everything."

Dong smiled and pulled Ai in, pressing their bodies together again in a tight hug. He didn't say anything else, he didn't need to. He knew that he and Ai were on the same page and any additional words now would just make the moment feel crowded. Having each other here under the moonlight was enough and would always be enough.

Dong didn't know how he knew exactly, but he had a strong feeling that he would never stop feeling that way. Ai was it for him, the person he'd been looking for all his life, the one for which his soul called.

Together they made their way inside, bringing the sheet along with them and tossing it to the side before crawling into bed. Ai produced another sheet from one of the chests of drawers and wrapped it around them as they nestled down to sleep.

The next morning came far too quickly for Dong's taste, especially because the Emperor didn't get to stop being the Emperor just because he was in town.

"If I had it my way." Ai whispered devilishly into Dong's ear as they lay together in bed, still naked from their activities the night before. "We would never leave this bed and I would spend all day worshiping you from head to toe."

Ai trailed kisses all the way down Dong's body, licking and nipping every few inches. Dong shivered and stretched finally waking up for the day, pouting as Ai pulled back. Rolling to his side, Dong watched as Ai wandered over to his boudoir and began rummaging through it for what he wanted to wear for the day. Dong bit his lip as he watched Ai's naked ass with desire, finally reaching down to cup his erection when Ai bent down, revealing a little more.

It wasn't unusual for Dong to wake up with morning wood, but after Ai's little show of implying that he wanted to spend all day fucking him into the mattress and then kissing all the way down his body, it was a little bit more than morning wood now. Raking his eyes over Ai, from his thick ass to his rippling back muscles, Dong began to leisurely stroke himself. Ai might have somewhere to be, but Dong was here as a guest and didn't need to be anywhere today, he might as well enjoy the view.

He rubbed his thumb over the leaking head and let out a small noise of pleasure, freezing as Ai stopped mid reach into the closet and turned over his shoulder slowly.

"Are you jerking off watching me get dressed?" Ai asked slowly, his eyes darkening with hunger.

"No." Dong replied with a shrug. "I'm jerking off watching you walk around naked."

Ai licked his lips and almost made a move toward the bed when there was a knock at the door, Dong glanced over but Ai didn't stop staring at him for one moment.

"What is it?" Ai asked through the wall.

"The dignitaries have arrived." A low male voice boomed through-Bolin.

Ai closed his eyes and sighed. "Thank you Bolin, I will be there momentarily."

With Bolin clearly remaining on the other side of the door, Dong began stroking himself again, leaking a little as he watched Ai's cock quickly filling with blood.

"You, are the devil." Ai pointed accusingly at Dong.

"Mmm." Dong vocalized both in agreement and pleasure as he could feel his heart rate picking up and his breathing become shallower.

Ai went back to his search for clothes, but this time just grabbing the first robe that he laid his hands on, his eyes never leaving Dong for one second. Something about the way that Ai was watching him hungrily just spurred Dong on, he tilted his head back, biting his lip and trying to be as quiet as he could as he knew that Bolin was likely just on the other side of the door.

Ai pulled the robe over his head and began tying the sash around his waist. He was just about ready to walk out the door and Dong wanted to finish with Ai's eyes on him. So he didn't try to fight the building of pressure in his abdomen, he didn't fight his hand as it sped up, twisting slightly as it got to the head, and certainly didn't stop his words from tumbling from his mouth as he felt himself tip over the edge.

"Fuck- Ai..." Dong mumbled as he came all over his hand. Before he could say anything else, Ai had closed the distance between them in the room and stolen his mouth in a deep and wanting kiss.

"That, you asshole," Ai growled against his lips before pulling back and making his way to the door. "Is going to give me blue balls for the rest of the day."

"Good." Dong smirked, sitting up in bed. "Maybe I will help you deal with them when you get back."

Dong saw Ai shiver and adjust himself from across the room. "You fucking better."

Dong chuckled to himself and looked down at his hand, starting to formulate a plan for the morning when he heard Ai again.

"Hey." Dong looked up and Ai's expression had melted into one of fondness.

"Hey." Dong replied.

"I love you." Ai smiled, seeming even happier when Dong broke out into a blush.

"I love you, too." Dong smiled shyly and Ai laughed quietly under his breath.

"Really? All that and now you get embarrassed?" Ai turned the knob. "What am I going to do with you?"

Ai shot him one more blinding smile before cracking the door a little and slipping out, closing it behind him. Dong fell back onto the bed and brought his hands up to cover his face, immediately pulling them away and cringing a little. He'd forgotten there was cum on his hand and now, there was cum on his face. Lovely.

That meant, it was time for a bath. Dong rolled out of bed and padded over to the private bath; not having put on any clothes last night, he was able to just walk directly into the water. Before getting to work cleaning himself up, Dong allowed himself to just relax in the warmth of the hot spring.

The last few days had been an absolute whirlwind but he was happier than he'd ever been before. He needed to check in with Lihua and see how she was enjoying herself, but if her and Bolin's general absence were any indication, Dong thought she was probably enjoying herself just fine.

His life had changed drastically in the time span of just a couple of months. He'd gone from being a newly appointed official in a town that nobody knew about, in one of the smallest provinces in China, to being the lover of the Emperor and living in the palace...

Wait.

Dong ruffled his brows, was he living here? No, he was just visiting. Right? If he had moved fully they would have packed up their full home instead of just their clothes.

Or would they?

Dong chewed on the inside of his cheek as he thought. If they were to move into the palace, where would they even put all of their furniture? Dong would want to bring his books and he was sure that Lihua would want to bring her sewing equipment but there really wouldn't be a need for them to move all their furniture.

Dong felt himself blushing, sinking under the water to his eyes. He really needed to talk to Ai first, it was incredibly presumptuous of him to assume that Ai even wanted him to move in right now. Then, on top of that, what would happen with his job? Would he continue to work? Would he continue in the same capacity that he was in right now or would he be moved to a new position?

On the other hand, what would his life even look like if he didn't work? Growing up on the countryside, there was never a moment when he wasn't doing something. If it wasn't going to school and helping out around the house, it would be making deliveries to and from the neighbors, and lending a hand wherever he could. Honestly, Dong didn't know what his days would even look like if he were to stop working.

After cleaning himself off, Dong grabbed a robe and dried off, heading over to the boudoir. Ai had insisted that he unpack instead of living out of his luggage while he was visiting, and since he would be spending a majority of his time in Ai's quarters, it made the most sense for him to put his clothes there. After getting dressed, Dong meandered over to the door and left the room, wandering out into the gardens.

If he was going to be the live-in-lover to the Emperor, he might as well figure out what his days would look like.

First, Dong swung by the dining hall to see if there was any food around. Unfortunately, it seemed that Ai and the dignitaries were eating elsewhere, so there was no food set out. Following his nose however, Dong made his way down a hallway off the main dining hall and found himself in one of the kitchens. Doing a quick scan of the space, there didn't seem to be anything major going on, but Dong did catch sight of a chef working on something, presumably prep for lunch.

"Excuse me." Dong tried, walking further into the kitchen. The chef looked up in question and his eyebrows ruffled in confusion. "Sorry to bother you, I was just looking for some breakfast. Do you know where I might get some?"

The chef opened his mouth for a moment before closing it and holding up a finger. "Hang on."

Dong watched as the man wandered over to a bamboo basket that was steaming over boiling water and reached in, dropping a couple of fluffy looking food items on a plate.

"Here." The chef slid the plate across the table and gestured for Dong to sit. "Some fresh baozi."

"Thank you." Dong's mouth was watering just from looking at them, so with no further pomp and circumstance, he sat down and began to eat. After a few moments, a cup of tea was placed on the table beside him and he looked back up, smiling gratefully. The man began preparing another plate and cup of tea and for a moment, Dong thought he might join him for breakfast. But then the man just placed the set up down on the counter next to Dong and went back to what he was doing.

Dong was about to ask when he heard footsteps coming down the hallway. He turned over his shoulder just in time to see a woman in dark red and gold robes enter the space.

"Lin." The woman's voice was singsongy and carried across the room without too much noise on her part. "Who is this?"

The chef looked up from what he was doing and glanced over at Dong before turning his attention back to the woman.

"Apologies your Grace, I thought he was with you."

Your Grace?

Dong looked back and forth between the two for a moment contemplating if he should leave or not when the woman sighed, planting her hands on her hips.

"Well, I suppose there is no harm in it." The lovely woman made her way across the room and planted herself in the seat right next to Dong. She reached over and took the cup of tea, taking a sip from it before turning her attention to Dong.

"As long as you're not expecting manners of any caliber. I come in here so that I can eat in peace."

Dong shook his head and took another bite out of his bao. "No expectations here. I'm pretty out of place in the palace anyway, so I don't know that I'd even be able to recognize let alone call you on poor manners if you exhibited them."

The woman looked Dong up and down warily for a moment before, Dong supposed, deeming his answer satisfactory, pushing up her sleeves and taking the baozi in her hand, taking a large bite.

"They are very good." Dong addressed the chef, realizing that he hadn't complimented the food since sitting down. Lin nodded and allowed a small smile to spread across his face before returning back to what he was doing.

"Lin is the best chef we have here at the palace." The woman said matter of factly. "He primarily cooks for the servants and consorts but I always liked his food much better than the fancy stuff they serve during official events."

"You're too kind." Lin did not look up from what he was doing but Dong swore that he could see a blush appearing across his cheeks.

"That makes a lot of sense." Dong mused, taking a closer look at the baozi. "I was just wondering why this food reminded me of home. I didn't really think about it earlier, but now that you mention it, this really does taste similar to the bao that my mom would make during the summer for us after we had done our morning chores."

It could have been his imagination, but Dong swore that he saw the woman's shoulders relax a little at the mention of his home.

"I also come from a very small town." The woman spoke up, taking another bite. "Growing up I always helped my mom with the cooking while my brothers helped tend to the farm. They would get up before the sun did and do their morning chores, then by the time they were done, mom and I were finished cooking and we would all have breakfast together."

Dong nodded. "It's very strange being here. Not necessarily bad, just different."

The woman stared at her bao for a couple of moments, a sort of sad look drawing across her face. "That's true. I used to hate it here when I first arrived, but I've managed to find some positive things about it, I think. Like coming and eating breakfast in here sometimes with Lin."

Dong finished the last of his bao and thanked Lin who had come to top off their tea.

"The gardens are beautiful." Dong said taking another sip from his fresh tea.

"They are." The woman agreed, nodding along. "I try to tend to some of the finickier flowers when I can, but that's not always possible, the servants will sometimes scold me for getting my hands dirty."

She laughed lightly, a soft tinkling noise that carried its way through the kitchen and flew away out the window. "I think that some of them forget that I've been tending to gardens since before some of them were born."

Dong nodded. "I remember when I first came here, to the capital. It was for a conference, I'd recently gotten my position and I remember being so absolutely awestruck by the way that everything looked here. It was so different."

The woman nodded, "So you were here to meet with A- the Emperor then?"

"Sort of." Dong took another sip of tea. "Technically I wasn't supposed to be meeting directly with him, but I accidentally ran into him in the library without knowing who he was."

The woman turned her head, her mouth slightly open, looking at him with amusement and disbelief.

"You're Dong Xian aren't you?"

Dong looked over and met her gaze. "Yes- but who are you?"

The woman covered her mouth with one hand and her shoulders began to shake. It started off small but slowly became bigger and bigger as her laughter grew. At this point, even Lin was looking over, a wide-eyed look on his face. Dong was just about to ask what was so funny when the woman's laughter finally subsided and she took a deep breath, smile still plastered on her face.

"It seems your strange luck continues, Dong." The woman tilted her head, looking over at him. "My name is Zhao Feiyan, I am Ai's wife, and the Empress of China."

16

Chapter Sixteen

"My name is Zhao Feiyan, I am Ai's wife, and the Empress of China."

Those words echoed through Dong's mind for what seemed like an eternity. The second time started moving again, Dong immediately choked on his tea, coughing violently into his arm.

"Are you alright?" Feiyan leaned over to check and Dong fought his very hardest to get it together. Why did this keep happening to him? Had he pissed off a god in a past life? It seemed as though he was just destined to look like an absolute idiot in front of everyone important he would ever meet.

"I'm fine." Dong choked out, focusing on breathing slowly. Sitting up straight again, he took another sip of tea to calm the cough and collected himself before turning back to Feiyan. "You know who I am?"

Dong hadn't meant for that to be the first question he asked his lover's wife but frankly he was so surprised that she had known his name that he couldn't think of anything else. Feiyan looked surprised for a moment before she began to laugh, only thinking to hide her mouth as an afterthought.

"I'm sorry." Feiyan apologized when the laughter subsided. "It's just, you are exactly as Bolin described to me, I really should have picked up on it earlier."

Dong adjusted the cup of tea in his hands, unsure what to do with that information. As if sensing his questions, Feiyan gestured for Lin to come and fill up their tea again, indicating to Dong that she wanted to speak more. He had no concept of the appropriate manners to have when meeting your lover's wife, but at the very least, she didn't seem to hate him, so that was comforting.

"You don't seem to understand the gravity of your position." Feiyan continued, leaning a little onto the counter. "Most men- well, most people really, would be overly aware of the power they held in your place."

Dong frowned and brought the teacup to his lips again remembering something Ai had mentioned to him a long time ago when they were relaxing in the garden. He had said something about how most people in his position would be taking advantage of being so close to the Emperor. Something about that hadn't really sat right with Dong at the time and he'd brushed it off as a little over cautiousness on Ai's part but it seemed that Ai hadn't been exaggerating.

"Ai said something like that to me once." Dong mused. "I never understood. Why does it matter that he's the Emperor? If anything, I'm the lucky one for being able to be with him all this time."

Feiyan made a small noise of approval and took another sip of her tea before continuing. "Well, aside from the fact that you are so close to the Emperor, Ai doesn't really choose to have people in his orbit. The fact that you spent every night with him the week that you were here for the conference was a big deal. Even with his lovers, he very rarely has repeats, switching up the person every night."

Dong felt his face begin to heat up, both because of what his being around Ai so often meant about what Ai had felt for him even early on and the fact that it was just now dawning on him that the Empress, Feiyan, also known as Ai's wife, was very well informed about the fact that he and Ai were sleeping together regularly.

"Don't be embarrassed." Feiyan waved her hand, putting down her cup. "I've known about you since the first time you spent the night in Ai's room. We don't interact much but he's still my husband and I try to keep tabs on him as best I can."

Dong looked over at Feiyan with awe, she was kinder than he'd expected. When Ai had told him how much his wife allegedly disliked him, he'd half expected that she would be hostile whenever he was brought up, but it seemed the opposite almost. It seemed like she did care, but was careful to give him his space.

"He and I never had a romantic relationship, I don't know if he told you, but I was already betrothed to someone else when he chose me to be his wife. It wasn't his fault, he didn't know, but I know that he still blames himself. My parents should have told him about my previous engagement but they were too excited that the Emperor wanted to marry their daughter."

"I'm sorry." Dong replied, his thumb making its way around the lip of the teacup. "I can only imagine how difficult that must have been for you."

Feiyan smiled sadly. "It's alright, Ai was kind enough to let him come visit whenever he could. In fact, recently, he even put in for a transfer to allow him to come live at the palace with me. He truly is the kindest person that I've ever met and I don't know that I could have gotten any luckier with this marriage."

"I think-" Dong started, hesitating. He wasn't quite sure that it was his place to make this observation but Feiyan seemed kind enough and he hated seeing Ai upset, so maybe it would be alright in this instance. "I think maybe you should talk to him about all of this."

Feiyan raised her eyebrows but didn't interrupt him or accuse him of sticking his nose into things that were none of his business so Dong continued.

"He may have mentioned to me in the past that he was under the impression that you resented him to the point of hating him."

Feiyan opened her mouth in shock, forgetting to cover it with her hand for a moment. She put down her teacup and turned her body so that it was facing Dong.

"Really? He thinks I hate him?" Feiyan's forehead was creased with worry and something clenched in Dong's heart for the Empress. She had been trying so hard to be the best Empress she could be, she hadn't considered that Ai might have been more worried about her situation than she was. "I always thought that it would be easier for him if I did my duties as the Empress without leaning on him too much, especially because he knew how dedicated I was to my relationship. But maybe I was wrong..."

"I wouldn't worry too much." Dong piped up again. He wasn't quite sure where he was getting all this confidence to give advice on what Ai would want, but for some reason, he felt like he knew, at least a little, how Ai might react if he were in this situation with them right now. "I think if you just talk to him and clear things up, you'll both feel better."

Dong took another sip of his tea and put it on the counter, looking over at Feiyan who was watching him, a soft expression on her face.

"You truly are an incredible person, Dong." Feiyan confessed. "I haven't spent more than an hour with you and I can already tell that you are a kind hearted person who cares deeply and would never even think about taking advantage of someone for your own personal gains."

Dong opened his mouth to protest but was met with Feiyan's hand and a shake of her head. "The fact that you are about to tell me that you're not all that just solidifies what I already think. You're just the kind of person that Ai needs in his life."

Dong looked down into his tea blushing slightly. He knew that even if he argued more, he wouldn't win, Feiyan was fiery and determined.

So instead Dong settled on, "Thank you."

"Dong?" The pair at the counter turned towards the entrance to the kitchen as a distinctly female voice made its way down the hall, Dong recognized it immediately.

"I'm in here Lihua." Turning back to Feiyan, he explained. "My wife."

The Empress lifted her eyebrows. "She knows?"

"Of course." Dong replied as Lihua made her way into the kitchen.

"There you are." Lihua made her way over to the pair stopping next to the counter. "Bolin mentioned that you might have wandered off to get food after waking up so I thought I'd join you."

Dong smiled and nodded. "Feiyan, this is Lihua, my wife. Lihua, this is Feiyan, Ai's wife."

Lihua smiled and bowed before doing a double take. "I'm sorry. Ai's wife? Like 'the Empress of China' Ai's wife?"

"Pleasure to meet you." Feiyan grinned, bowing her head slightly.

Lihua smacked Dong in the arm, shooting him a terrifying look. "Why didn't you start with that?" She hissed.

"Please don't worry about it." Feiyan replied laughing a little. "Dong and I were just bonding over breakfast, please, join us."

Feiyan gestured to the seat next to her and from the corner of his eye, Dong saw that Lin was already preparing a plate and teacup for Lihua, who sat down gingerly next to Feiyan.

"Thank you, your highness."

"Feiyan, please." The Empress waved her hand in front of her face. Dong hadn't expected her to be as nonchalant about titles as she was but he supposed that it made sense given where she came from. "I love your robe, you must tell me where you got it." Feiyan gushed, now getting a closer look at what Lihua was wearing.

"Oh!" Lihua blushed and looked at Dong for help.

"Lihua actually made it herself." Dong said proudly, receiving an impressed look from Feiyan and an embarrassed one from Lihua. "She makes most of our clothes and certainly all of my favorite ones."

Feiyan's eyes lit up and she turned back to Lihua taking her hands in her own. "You simply must make something for me too. Please?"

"I- of course!" Lihua stuttered.

"Oh, thank you!" Feiyan let go of Lihua's hands and relaxed a little back into her seat. "Everything that they make me here is in the style of what's popular in the capital and they won't let me wear the robes I brought from home because they're too plain. But if you were to make me some custom robes in that style, I'm sure they wouldn't be able to protest."

Lihua's eyes lit up and she looked over at Dong, making eye contact in a way that Dong understood very well. She was asking him if this could possibly be real. He nodded and finished his tea as the two of them continued talking and planning out future designs for Feiyan. Dong waved off Lin as he moved to refill his tea and stood up, bowing slightly at the hip.

"Well ladies, I'm going to take my leave now, you two certainly sound like you have a lot to talk about."

Feiyan turned around, excitement painted across her face. "Yes! We certainly do!"

As Dong had Feiyan's attention, Lihua mouthed the words 'thank you' and Dong nodded, smiling back at his wife. In a moment the Empress's attention was back on Lihua and Dong took the opportunity to nod thankfully at Lin and sneak out the way he'd come in.

Once outside, he gave himself the opportunity to laugh, at nothing in particular, just how he found his morning going. It was surreal almost, waking up in Ai's bed, getting breakfast with the Empress of China, and running into his wife as she and Feiyan became fast friends. Dong took off in the direction of the library, he hadn't really decided what he was going to do yet today when he met Feiyan in the kitchen for breakfast but he'd been burning to go back to the library since he got here and it seemed like the perfect time.

It didn't take him very long to arrive at the library and when he stepped in, someone putting books back on the shelves took notice and bowed gracefully. Dong returned the gesture and made his way further inside and out of sight. Last time he was here, nobody had noticed him, but now it seemed as though everyone knew who he was. Dong turned a corner around a bookshelf and was hit with an all too familiar sight.

The light was different and this time he was truly alone but there was no mistaking it. It was here that he'd met Ai, at the time he hadn't realized how much that moment was going to change his life but now looking back, he recognized that first decision of walking into the library as the moment. Wandering over to the table, Dong pulled out the seat and sat down, putting himself in the spot Ai had sat all those months ago.

The sun was trickling through the window warming his back and Dong chuckled. Sitting here now, he really couldn't fault Ai for having fallen asleep sitting here, it really was the perfect napping spot. But, he'd just woken up and didn't want to be lulled back to sleep so instead of giving in, he got up and wandered back to the front to ask the book-keeper where the poetry books were.

The gentleman had been very helpful and led Dong back through the maze of shelves and over to a section fairly close to the napping spot. After making sure that he didn't need any assistance in his browsing, the man bowed again and took his leave, back up to the front. Dong turned his attention over to the shelf, scanning the titles.

There truly were considerably more books of poetry than he could have ever dreamed of and it took all of his willpower not to pull them all off the shelves and sit down right there in the walkway. So instead, Dong pulled a couple off the shelf and made his way back to the table, sitting on the opposite side of the napping spot and got to making his way through the first book.

Many hours and four books later, Dong had made his way back to Ai's chambers and was currently sprawled out on the bed, snacking on something he had stolen from the kitchen after having forgotten to eat lunch and reading yet another book he'd plucked from the shelf. This one was particularly interesting because it seemed to be both a book of poetry and full of some sort of mnemonic devices used to memorize all the medicinal herbs that could be found growing around the country.

He'd made it to the L's when he heard the door creak open, raising his head from the book, he watched as Ai made his way in, closing the door quietly. Dong put the book down and sat up.

"Are you done with the dignitaries today?"

Ai's back was to him and he was being uncharacteristically quiet. Dong was about to ask again when Ai responded.

"You- you spoke to Feiyan today."

It wasn't a question, but rather a soft confirmation. Dong immediately got up and began walking over to Ai. Had he crossed a line? Should he not have spoken to her? Of course not! That was incredibly stupid of him to assume that Ai would just be fine with it.

"Ai- I'm sorry I should have waited until you were- ah." Dong had just reached Ai when the Emperor turned around and pulled him into a tight embrace, burying his face in Dong's neck.

"You have nothing to apologize for." Ai murmured softly. "She found me after my meetings today, said that you two talked, and- I'm so relieved."

Dong wasn't sure exactly what Ai was talking about but nevertheless, he brought his arms up and embraced his lover.

"I thought she hated me." Ah, Dong relaxed, rubbing Ai's back and truly taking in the complete feeling of intense relief that washed over the Emperor.

"She never hated you." Dong cooed.

"I thought- I don't think I could have- I'm so glad. I didn't think she would ever forgive me, so I never gave myself the opportunity to forgive myself."

Ai pulled back, keeping his hands anchored on Dong's shoulders.

"You did that. For me." Ai's eyes were rimmed with tears.

Dong ran his fingers through Ai's hair lovingly. "I really didn't do that much."

"No." Ai took Dong's cheeks in his hands and placed their foreheads together. "Don't do that."

Their eyes met and Dong stopped. He'd known how much everything with Feiyan had bothered him, so of course he wanted to help clear things up. But before he continued to protest, he stopped, remembering Feiyan's words at breakfast.

You are just the kind of person that Ai needs in his life.

Right, Ai was the Emperor and always had people coming to him for the things that they needed, leaning on him, and always taking. He had never really had anyone there to truly look after him, to watch his back and make sure he was alright. Bolin did the best he could but there was only so much that someone in his position could do.

Dong pushed Ai's hair out of his face and touched their lips together softly. "I'd do anything for you Ai." Dong whispered against Ai's lips.

The taller man pulled him in, arms wrapped around his back and together they stood that way for longer than Dong could keep count. Not that he would ever want to, the moments that he spent with Ai were the happiest that he'd ever had in his life and if he had it his way, they would go on forever.

17

Chapter Seventeen

"What happened to that promise you made me this morning, hm?" Ai shifted so his breath tickled the cuff of Dong's ear. "Was that all talk or were you still planning on helping me out with that?"

Dong chuckled and let himself be backed up onto the bed. "I don't know, why don't you find out your Highness?"

Ai smiled and pressed their lips together. Despite the teasing tone, Ai kept things light, taking his time kissing Dong deeply and gently guiding him onto his back. Despite nothing being specifically different, Dong could tell that Ai had something on his mind, even so, he wasn't one to push it. So instead of asking, he followed Ai's lead and continued on at a slow, sensual pace. Their limbs tangled among the sheets and with each other and slowly but surely, the clothes began coming off, getting discarded without a second glance to the side.

Dong rolled them so that he was on top and began his journey kissing Ai's jaw and down his neck to his broad chest. Experimentally, Dong flicked out his tongue against one of the Emperor's pert nipples and was rewarded with a groan of pleasure.

While the other times had been fast and almost frantic, this time, they kissed at a leisurely pace. Slowly warming each other up. Dong could tell that Ai wanted to go further by the jerky movements of his hips as he sought out friction but the Emperor was still holding back for some reason. So instead, Dong pressed open mouth kisses to Ai's neck before finding his pulse point and sucking. He knew that it would probably leave a mark, but he also knew that he didn't really care. Ai loved it when he left marks and who was he to deny the man he loved anything that he wanted?

Slowly, Dong lowered his body down on top of Ai, both of them gasping as their erections bumped together. Instinctively, Dong's hand found its way down between them and grasped their lengths together giving them a cursory stroke. This pulled a relieved sigh from Ai and he seemed to relax a little into the touch, but as the ministrations began to speed up, Ai grabbed Dong's wrist.

"Wait." Immediately Dong let go and brought both hands up to cup Ai's face.

"What is it?" Dong could sense that they were about to talk about the reason that Ai had seemed a little bit off, but he honestly wasn't sure what it could be. "You know you can tell me anything."

Ai's cheeks flushed a little and he stubbornly dodged Dong's gaze, looking into the corner. "I know that- it's just..."

Dong didn't push, he just lay there with him, running his fingers through Ai's beautiful hair and pressing a kiss to his face every now and then.

"I-I want..." Ai began tentatively.

"Anything, tell me what you want baby."

Then with resolve set in his jaw, blush still burning across his cheeks, Ai brought his gaze bashfully back to meet Dong's.

"I want you to do me tonight." If possible, Ai's cheeks got even redder but he did not look away, a determined air about him now.

"You- really?" Dong was nearly speechless, he hadn't even considered this as something that Ai would want since he'd never shown interest in it before.

"Yes." Ai nodded, a little more sure of himself.

"You've never wanted to before, so I thought-"

"I know." Ai replied, covering Dong's hand with one of his own. "I've never- I've always been on the giving end, but... if it's with you- I want to. I trust you."

Dong thought his heart might burst at Ai's confession. He buried his face in Ai's neck and nodded.

"Yes. Anything for you." Ai wrapped his arms around him and breathed a sigh of relief. Dong could feel the tension draining from Ai's body as they lay there together, all the previous hesitation and weirdness gone.

Pulling back, Dong brushed his lips against the cuff of Ai's ear.

"Relax and let me take care of you, okay?" Ai nodded and Dong claimed his lips again, pressing a couple of kisses there before moving the train of kisses down Ai's neck and chest, working his way down to the Emperor's stomach. Dong settled himself between Ai's legs and continued to shower him with kisses and love bites all over the Emperor's thighs and hips. Dong could see Ai's length bobbing, neglected between his legs; slowly Dong brought his hand up, massaging Ai's balls before sliding his grip up to his leaking cock.

Ai's breath hitched as Dong wiped his thumb over the head, letting the precum leak down the full length. After getting his hand a little bit more lubed up, Dong leaned over, taking the tip in his mouth and leisurely stroking the shaft. Dong remembered the first time he'd received and he wanted to make sure that this experience was as enjoyable and special for Ai as possible. So, he made sure to focus on Ai's dick, at a speed that spurred on the Emperor's arousal but didn't let him get too close to the edge.

Dong paused his ministrations to reach over to the bottle of lubricant sitting on the table next to them. Quickly he popped off the top and covered the fingers on his right hand, rubbing the extra over his own aching erection. He hissed as he stroked himself but stopped after the lubricant was distributed, this moment wasn't about him, it was about Ai and he intended to keep it that way.

Using his tongue to circle the head of Ai's cock, he distracted the other man as he slid his hand between Ai's cheeks, playing at the hole. He watched carefully for any sign of discomfort from Ai, but only received moans of pleasure. So gently, he pressed the pad of his finger against Ai's hole, pleasantly surprised as he met less resistance than he thought he would. Despite this being Ai's first time, the way that he sucked Dong's finger inside, really seemed like this was something he'd been thinking about and wanting for quite some time.

Dong would have smiled had his mouth not been occupied. So instead he hummed happily, eliciting a shiver from Ai as the vibrations traveled down his cock. Slowly pumping his finger, Dong began to work it deeper and deeper until he was fully up to his knuckle. Ai whined as he paused and began rocking his hips back against Dong's hand encouraging him to continue.

Dong licked up the side of Ai's cock and buried his face in his crotch, pressing kisses and licks to the base as he worked in another finger. His free hand itched to touch his cock but he knew that he couldn't, he needed to be able to last inside of Ai and if he touched himself beforehand he would burst immediately upon sinking into that tight heat. So instead, Dong wrapped his free arm around Ai's thigh, cupping his ass.

Ai moaned, half in pleasure and half in discomfort.

"I know baby. I know, but you're doing so good." Dong cooed, pausing the movements of his fingers and refocusing his attention back on Ai's cock. He knew that the stretch could be a lot so he rotated his wrist back and forth slowly to allow Ai to get used to the slight burn of the new girth inside of him.

Ai tilted his hips back, pressing Dong's fingers further inside him. Dong switched off between sucking at the tip of Ai's cock and murmuring encouragement and praise as he let Ai take control of the pace for a moment.

"Keep going." Ai sounded more fucked out than Dong had ever heard him before and despite the newness, the tone of his voice and the lust dripping from his gaze, Dong's heart squeezed at how much Ai clearly wanted this. Nodding, Dong began working his fingers in and out, scissoring them a little, prepping Ai for the third finger. After a couple of minutes, Ai seemed to have worked past the burn, now just moaning without abandon.

Encouraged, Dong pressed his fingers in further and flipped his wrist, searching for the bundle of nerves that he knew would make Ai scream.

As his fingers dragged over a specific area, Dong grinned to himself, as Ai's back arched off the bed and he gasped.

"Oh, gods…" Ai gripped the sheets until his knuckles were white with exertion, his breath picking up even more. "Dong, if you keep doing that, I'm going to cum…"

"Good." Dong continued rubbing the spot and kissing up and down Ai's torso until Ai gently took his arm in his hand.

"No. I want to cum with you inside of me." Dong felt his cock throb at the confession. Ai looked bashful but determined, gazing lovingly up at him.

"Anything for you." Dong murmured. Readjusting, he slowed his pace, focusing on the stretch and dotting kisses up and down Ai's thighs. He remembered the first time he'd ever received, it had been both incredible and overwhelming, so he wanted to make this as easy and pleasureful for Ai as possible.

He slid a third finger in slowly, avoiding Ai's pleasure center as much as he could, but even with just the thrust of Dong's fingers inside of him, Ai tossed back his head and moaned loudly, tilting his hips back and starting to fuck himself on Dong's fingers. It was so sexy, Dong couldn't help himself as he rutted into the sheets slightly just to relieve some of the pressure that was building. He had never heard Ai make those noises before and if he thought that being dominated by the other man was sexy, it had nothing on the desperate mewls and pleas slipping from Ai's lips as he resigned himself to Dong's mercy.

After a little longer, Dong buried his face in Ai's hip.

"Fuck." He cursed. "I don't know how much longer I can hold back, do you think you can take me, baby?"

"Dong." Dong lifted his head at the mention of his name and was greeted with Ai's loving and fucked out gaze. "Make love to me."

"Yes, okay." Dong nodded, slowly retracting his fingers. Ai whimpered at the sudden emptiness but would not need to wait much longer. Shifting forward onto his knees, Dong took a pillow and propped it up under Ai's hips to make it easier on his back. He knew that it would be easier to do this from behind, but neither of them wanted that right now. Leaning over, Dong took Ai's lips in a passionate kiss, cupping his cheek tenderly, and moaning softly as his erection bumped up against Ai's ass.

He was still lubed from earlier but just to make sure everything went smoothly, Dong took the bottle from the bedside table and uncorked it again, pouring a little more into his hand. Leaning forward again, Dong kissed Ai, his tongue exploring inside the Emperor's mouth as he shuddered, stroking the extra lubrication over his painfully hard length.

"You ready?" Dong asked, pressing the head of his cock up against Ai's entrance.

"Yes." Ai took Dong's face between his hands and pressed their foreheads together. Dong started pressing in, both of their breaths hitching as the head caught and began sinking in. Dong had to focus harder than he'd ever focused before not to climax on the spot. Ai was squeezing him and panting into his mouth, he had no idea how he was going to last once he got all the way inside. But he knew that he had to try for Ai, the love of his life.

Taking a deep breath, Dong began pushing forward, sinking further and further in, relishing the way that Ai's thighs began to shake as he took each inch. Then finally, after what seemed like forever, Dong's hips met Ai's ass and he was fully sheathed.

Dong bit down on his lower lip as Ai clenched around him, it felt too good, it was so different from how they'd done it before and he felt almost overwhelmed at the new sensations. But then, just like always, Ai's touch brought him back. He ran his fingers up and down Dong's sides almost as if he sensed that he needed the grounding.

"How does it feel?" Dong asked, pressing kisses to Ai's forehead and cheeks.

"Mmm." Ai vocalized happily. "Feels full, 'm feels good." He slurred, seemingly drunk off of the feeling of his lover filling him up.

Dong chuckled, running his fingers through Ai's hair. "I'm going to move now, okay?"

Ai nodded and Dong took a deep breath before pulling out partway and rocking his hips forward to re-sheathe himself. They both let out a moan, filling the room with their sounds as Dong repeated his motion, this time pulling out a little more until he found a rhythm. It wasn't fast or hard as they sometimes liked, but rather slow and full of affection and love.

This wasn't a fuck. This was a promise made between partners that they would always be there. A promise that said, *I'm yours forever, no matter what could ever happen, no matter what the world may throw our way.* A promise that Dong had never made to anyone and knew in his heart that he would never make again. Ai was it for him. Everything that he had been looking for, everything he never knew that he needed, and everything he could ever possibly want.

"Ai-" Dong panted, rolling his hips. "I love you."

"Ah..." Ai gripped Dong's back, wrapping his legs around his lover's torso. "I love you, too... more than anyone."

"Me too." Dong kissed up to Ai's shoulder and buried his face in the crook of his neck. "I've never loved anyone like I love you. You- ah... you are the love of my life."

Ai moaned louder, rocking his hips back into Dong's to match his thrusts. Dong wrapped one arm around Ai's waist, pulling him close and tilting his hips slightly. The next time he snapped his hips forward, Ai gasped and Dong grinned to himself.

"Fuck. Do that again." Ai begged and Dong was more than happy to oblige. Burying his face in Ai's neck, Dong focused on hitting that spot over and over again, quickly becoming overwhelmed by the feeling of Ai clenching around him. The friction became almost too much, it had been such a long time since Dong had topped that he was surprised that he'd lasted this long already.

"Oh, gods- Dong." Ai swore, his thighs shaking as he wrapped his legs around Dong's body. "I'm so close, please..."

Ai's begging was almost enough to send Dong over the edge himself but he was determined to leave Ai fully satisfied first. Despite the building heat in his belly, his balls tightening up and drawing in against him, Dong captured Ai's mouth in his and focused on hitting that spot over and over again until Ai was sobbing in pleasure. Dong reached in between them and wrapped his hand around Ai's weeping cock, stroking him only a couple of times before Ai was seizing up, shooting his seed between them.

Dong could have sobbed in relief as Ai clenched around him, ripping his own orgasm out of him. He only had to thrust one more time before he was cumming, hard, emptying his load into Ai. His shoulders shook with exertion, his orgasm seemingly lasting forever as it went on and on, impossibly long. Finally, Dong collapsed on top of the Emperor, holding him close and burying his face in Ai's sweaty neck, peppering his skin with kisses.

Ai held onto him, tracing patterns into his back and humming happily as they both came down from their climaxes.

"Is this what it's like for you all the time?" Ai asked with an amused air to his voice.

Dong chuckled weakly and lifted his head to press a kiss to Ai's cheek. "Usually. Though it really does depend on the partner, with you? Absolutely."

Ai hummed in response and played gently with a lock of Dong's hair. "I've clearly been missing out."

"I'm so happy you enjoyed it." Dong replied, smiling into Ai's neck. "Thank you, for trusting me with this."

Ai took Dong's face in his hands and pulled him back so that he could look into his eyes. "There is no one else that I would ever have trusted this with."

Dong smiled and leaned down, lightly kissing Ai's lips. "I love you."

"I love you, too." Ai replied. "More than anything."

Dong shifted, feeling himself soften, and chuckled to himself as Ai grimaced as he slipped out.

"Before you ask, yes." Dong smiled, recognizing what Ai was feeling. "Feeling it dripping out of you is the worst part."

"Oh, good." Ai joked. "I was just about to ask about that specifically."

"I know." Dong laughed. "That was probably the most alarming thing when I bottomed for the first time. For whatever reason, I didn't think about how it would feel coming out. Come on, let's take a bath."

Ai nodded and rolled to the edge of the bed to his feet. They walked together over to the private bath and Dong held Ai's hand, guiding him into the water. Once they were both submerged, Dong took his thumbs and massaged Ai's lower back gently.

"How's your back?"

"It's alright." Ai wrapped his arms around Dong's shoulders and leaned into him, enjoying the massage. "Doesn't really hurt, it's just sore more than anything else."

"Mmm, good." Dong continued rubbing Ai's back, turning his head to press kisses into his cheek and neck. He was glad, that meant that he'd prepped Ai properly. Anytime someone was bottoming for the first time they were bound to be sore, but he shouldn't be in pain if Dong had done his job right. "Tell me if anything starts to hurt okay?"

"Of course." Ai turned his head, lightly kissing Dong on the lips. "How did I get so lucky? Hm?"

Dong laughed, pulling Ai into his lap. "I don't know what you're talking about. I'm the lucky one here."

Ai breathed out through his nose in amusement before kissing Dong deeply. Truly, if Dong had been told a year ago that he would be here, not only spending this kind of time with the Emperor, but being fully and truly head over heels in love and being loved in return, he never would have believed it. But now, he couldn't think of anything else that felt more right than being here, Ai in his arms, their bodies pressed together, and feeling more loved than he ever had felt before in his life.

Leisurely, the pair finished bathing, taking the time to wash each other's bodies and hair in an excuse to touch and caress, not that they needed one. Then, together, they made their way back out of the bath and into bed, holding each other lovingly until they drifted to sleep.

18

Chapter Eighteen

Dong woke to the feeling of the sun warming his face, trickling in from the windows. He reached out to pull Ai in and get some extra cuddling in this morning but found himself alone. Ai must have already gotten up, leaving Dong to sleep while he went off, taking care of his Emperorly duties. Dong stretched and rolled over onto his stomach, the silk sheets draping off of him, covering him only from the waist down.

It was an incredible morning and Dong felt more rested than he had in quite some time. So, deciding not to waste the morning, Dong rolled out of bed and threw on one of his robes, pulling his hair up into a bun. As he opened the door, he was met by a familiar face.

"Good morning, Dong." Bolin smiled at him. "Lihua is waiting for us in the dining hall, she wanted to help make some breakfast this morning."

Dong smiled, he loved Lihua's cooking, and while he thoroughly enjoyed the fancy palace food here, he did miss the rustic charm that came with the foods from his hometown.

"What a nice surprise." Dong smiled and began walking down the hallway, noticing that Bolin had fallen into step behind him, Dong slowed his pace and waited for the guard to catch up. "You know, you don't need to walk behind me, we are friends right?"

Bolin's eyebrows raised up for a moment before a flush found his cheeks. He nodded and fell into step beside Dong as they made their way to the dining hall.

"I had hoped so, but I wasn't sure what with- everything." Bolin made a gesture with his hand that looked all encompassing.

Dong chuckled. "Which part? Me being your boss's partner or you dating my wife?"

Bolin's face got even redder and he shrugged. "Both."

"Don't worry about it." Dong waved his hand in front of his face. "You were instrumental in helping Ai and I get our heads out of our asses and realize that we belonged together and for that alone, I think we are both indebted to you. Then in terms of Lihua," Dong saw out of the corner of his eye, Bolin chew his lip discreetly. "I'm just so happy that she's happy and being cared for the way that she deserves.

Lihua is an amazing woman and while I do love her, ours was an arranged marriage and I think that she always knew that I liked men more than women anyway. Even so, she stayed by my side and became one of my best friends. There is nobody that I can think of that I would trust with her more than you Bolin."

"I- thank you, Dong." Dong glanced over to Bolin and watched as the tension left his body.

"Do you know where Ai is this morning?" Dong asked as they continued down the hall.

"I don't actually." Bolin confessed, shrugging. "I planned on going with him but he instead asked that I wait for you to wake up and bring you to the dining hall. I imagine that he is going to meet us there."

"Hm." Dong mused, wondering what Ai could possibly be up to this morning that he wouldn't want Bolin there for. "Well alright. Have you had Lihua's baozi yet?"

Bolin shook his head. "This was the first time that she requested access to the kitchens. I think Ai spoke to her the other day about it and they decided that it would be nice to have a homemade breakfast."

Dong pursed his lips, amused at Ai's obvious plotting. What exactly he was planning, Dong had no idea, but he supposed they would find out soon.

When they arrived at the dining hall, Mei Lan was helping Lihua set up the table and immediately Dong was hit with the familiar smell of home. What he was not expecting, however, was for Feiyan to turn the corner and place more food on the table.

"Feiyan." Dong stopped, surprised.

"Your majesty." Bolin paused, seemingly equally caught off guard, and bowed.

"Good morning Dong, Bolin." Feiyan rearranged a couple of things on the table and walked over. "There is no need to bow Bolin, we are just having a family breakfast."

Bolin raised his head to Feiyan's smiling face, seemingly at a loss for words.

"Oh, come now." Feiyan continued. "You can't seriously think that we don't consider you family at this point, now do you?"

Dong looked over to Bolin and his heart melted as he saw the older man blinking rapidly, clearly holding back tears.

"Come on." Lihua appeared next to them and took Bolin and Dong by the arms, leading them to the table. "Feiyan was telling me that Ai has a surprise for us."

As they all got situated, Feiyan said something to Mei Lan and sent her off back into the kitchens before sitting down. Then, after a few minutes, as the tea was being poured, Mei Lan came back, Ai on her heels.

As Ai settled down in the seat next to Dong, he leaned over and stole Dong's lips in a loving, good morning kiss.

"I see you've been busy this morning." Dong mused. "I wonder what you could possibly have brought us all here to talk about."

Ai's face lit up, smiling from ear to ear. "Well, I suppose there is no sense in delaying it any longer. Frankly, I can't believe I kept it a secret for as long as I did."

Everyone around the table except Feiyan seemed confused at the confession and suddenly, Dong realized that Feiyan must have been in on whatever it was.

Ai cleared his throat and reached over under the table, taking Dong's hand. "I've spoken to Feiyan about this and decided that I want to extend an official invitation to you two to come live in the palace permanently."

Dong opened his mouth in surprise, looking over at Lihua. Her face also read surprise and interestingly enough, so did Bolin's.

"Really?" Dong felt his throat closing with emotion as he looked over at Ai, squeezing his hand back.

"Yes." Feiyan piped up. "Ai and I have discussed this with the royal architect and we have designed a separate palace on the grounds for you to move into in an official capacity. Obviously, this need not change the sleeping arrangements for you and Ai, Dong, but we thought that it might be nice to have your own space here."

"Of course, if you liked, Bolin could also move out of the guards' quarters and into the space as well." Ai added, garnering a surprised and bashful look from the guard.

"Really?" Dong asked, giddiness building in his chest as he thought about the fact that he would never again have to make the long trek to the capital to see Ai.

"Yes really." Ai smiled broadly.

"Would you really be alright with that?" Lihua piped up and as Dong looked over at her, he realized that she was not asking about the move, but rather, Bolin living with her in the new space.

"Of course." Dong replied without a second thought. "As long as I have space for my office I don't think I would have any other requests. I assume that since I would still be sleeping in Ai's quarters that my clothes would go there as well." Looking over to Ai, Dong received the confirmation he was looking for in the nod he received from the Emperor.

"Great." Feiyan piped up. "Now that everything is all settled, let's enjoy this breakfast that Lihua so kindly made for us."

Then without a second thought, the group fell into a comfortable conversation about logistics, timelines, and plans for the rest of the day. As they ate together, Dong reveled in the profound feeling of happiness and comfort that he now knew he would get to keep, and he had never felt luckier.

Dong shelved the last couple of books on the built-in shelf and stepped back to admire his handiwork. It had taken a couple of months of construction to finish the palace and then another week or so to pack up their home in the countryside and move everything into their new space. But with the help of the palace servants, it had taken considerably less time than it would have if they'd done it on their own.

When they'd told their families and of course Governor Li, the response had been ecstatic, especially when Dong had told them about his new position he'd been promoted to. Dong had been resistant to it all when Ai had first mentioned it, but after some conversation and... persuasion on the part of the Emperor, Dong had finally conceded.

The last couple of days had been dedicated to moving into the new space and getting settled. Most of Dong's things had been moved into Ai's quarters but as requested, Ai had made sure that Dong had a study in the new living quarters where he could work and keep all of his books. It had taken the better part of the day to move everything into the study and set it up the way that he liked it, but it was worth it.

As he stood back and admired his handiwork, he heard the door open. He didn't need to turn to know who it was but did anyway so that he could wrap his arms around Ai and greet him with a kiss.

"I see you finally unpacked the last of it." Ai mused, looking around. "Is everything the way you like it?"

"Mmm." Dong vocalized, wrapping his arms around the Emperor's neck. "It is now."

Ai smiled, his eyes twinkling, and as Dong ran his fingers through his beautiful raven hair, he felt like the luckiest man in the world.

"So," Ai murmured slyly. "What do you say we go break in the bed back in our room, hm?"

Dong laughed. "It's the same bed Ai, we've already broken it in."

"Yes." Ai shrugged. "But now it's ours."

"I think you're just looking for an excuse to get me naked." Dong teased, pressing himself up against his partner.

"Maybe." Ai smiled mischievously.

Dong laughed, kissing Ai lovingly. "Well come on then, that bed isn't going to break in itself."

Ai's laughter sounded like music to his ears and as they made their way back to their quarters, hand in hand, Dong reveled in the peace of knowing that there was no place else that he would rather be.

Books by Harlowe Savage

The Monarchs of Eros Series

Alexander

Emperor Ai

Hadrian

About Author

Harlowe Savage is a queer author dedicated to creating stories that depict queer romances with the same amount of spice and passion that readers get from their straight counterparts. She firmly believes that the gap between the amount of LGBTQIA+ erotica and heterosexual erotica in the mainstream is far too large and intends to rectify this through normalizing queer romance novels and increasing accessibility of the genre.

www.harlowesavage.com
instagram.com/harlowesavage/
tiktok.com/@harlowesavage